'At the horizon we'd find the sky had fallen off and we'd know no better than to keep on driving.'

In praise of *Sister*:

"A novella of love and redemption that hits both the head and the heart, written in Strickley's signature pitch-perfect prose. Read this story. Read this story because it is just so fucking good."

-Eric Freeze
Author of *Invisible Men*

"Sarah Anne Strickley's gorgeously rendered characters catch hold of us and break our hearts. Her voice is irresistible, infused with an unexpected mixture of toughness and warmth. *Sister* is a splendid novella you won't want to end."

-David Philip Mullins
Author of *The Brightest Place in the World*

"I'm hard-pressed to recall a character I've ever rooted for harder than Sarah Anne Strickley's SISTER, the heartbeat and protagonist of her novella of the same name. Frank, wise, and unabashedly feminist, Strickey's portrait of a complicated marriage brims with tenderness and nuance. From high school to hospice, SISTER is a beautiful, bruising, intimate work, equal parts hilarious and gutting."

-Tracy Manaster Alifanz
Author of *The Done Thing*

Sarah Anne Strickley

Sister

summer camp
PUBLISHING

Summer Camp Publishing is an independent publisher of fine works of poetry and prose, rooted in Appalachia and concerned with beautiful, thought-provoking inspections of our nuanced world.

Summer Camp Publishing
PO Box 472
Banner Elk, NC 28604
SummerCampPublishing.com
Email: SummerCampPublishing@Gmail.com

Cover Art: Matthew Taylor Wilson.
Interior Design: Brooks Rexroat for Summer Camp Publishing.
Editors: Ali Braenovich and Brooks Rexroat.

First edition.

ISBN: 978-1-7353637-4-5
Library of Congress Control Number: 2020951319
Printed in the United States of America.

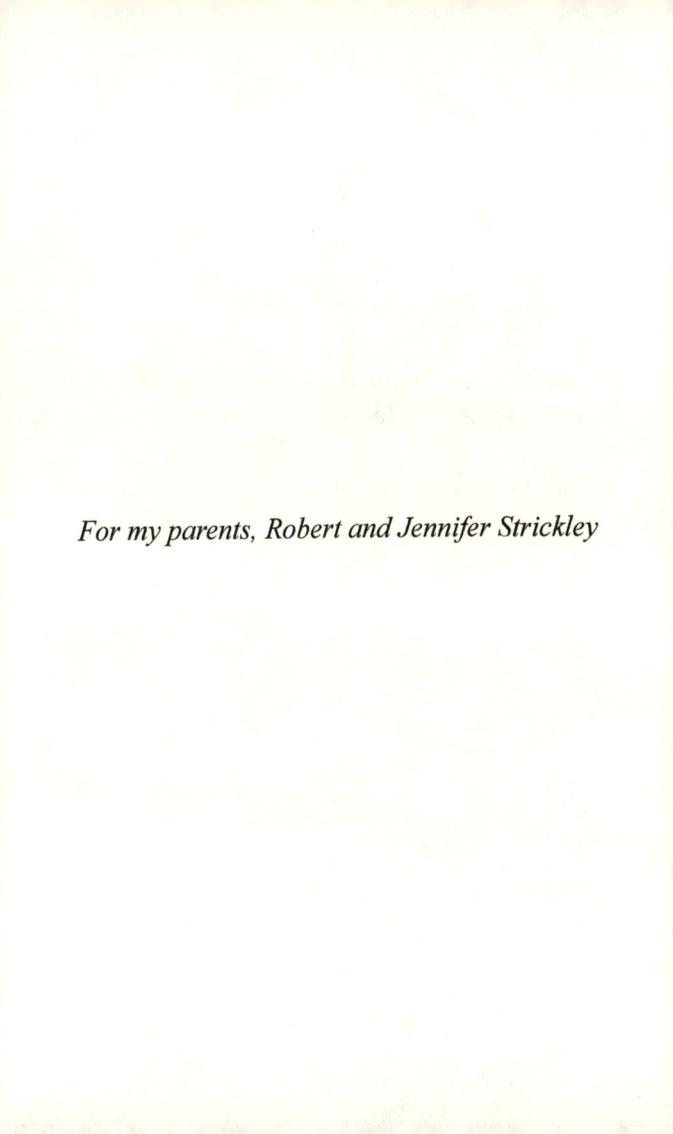

For my parents, Robert and Jennifer Strickley

"You used to say. 'Desire doubled is love and love doubled is madness.' / Madness doubled is marriage / I added."

        – from Ann Carson's *The Beauty of the Husband*

I.

It all started at the J.C. Penny's. It wasn't that I liked shopping there. I didn't. The only affordable ladies skirts and pants they sold all buttoned far too high on the waist and the whole place smelled of a strange, cottony cleanness that could only be manufactured because nothing real ever smells that clean, but the truth was that it was the only chain department store in Athens in the late 90s. And when you lived in a town as small as Athens, you sometimes started to wonder what the people in the real cities regarded as normal. What name brands were *they* doing these days? What was the new perfume, the best luggage? How high were heels? When you walked into the Penny's you got to walk into every Penny's everywhere and it could feel for a moment like you weren't where you really were, like you weren't so small. It was with an air of worldliness that I walked into that store—like I had money to waste, though it'd be clear to anyone looking that I didn't. My blouse was washing-machine grey. My jewelry was made of embroidery floss and plated gold.

I was probably more pleased than I should have been when the man in men's attire seemed to believe that I was a high priority customer, that I fully deserved his service and his attention. He emerged from the clothing racks as though he'd been stationed inside of them, standing at the ready. I told him I had a gift certificate I wanted to use on something nice for my husband. He took me straight to a ream of silk ties and asked me if my husband's suits had any subtle highlighting we might bring out with something contemporary, bold. I didn't have the nerve to tell him that my husband's suit wasn't subtle. It was only half a suit, a corduroy jacket he wore with black jeans when he went to weddings and funerals.

We went through three additional wheels of pricey ties, small-talking along the way. I shared a little about our lives, details I thought would be useful to share, while we considered the advantages and disadvantages of each tie and then moved on to the precious-metal cufflinks. It took half an hour for me to finally concede the defeat I'd known was coming since the first blue strip of silk turned softly in my hand: The man had shown me nothing that cost less than fifty dollars when I'd come in to spend twenty-five on good socks and underwear. "I had high hopes, but I don't see anything here he'd like," I said.

"Your husband must have very particular tastes."

"He does."

The man frowned, twisted his own maroon tie and then flung it over his shoulder. "I'm not a very good salesman, am I?" he asked. "We've spent all this time and I couldn't sell you on a single damn thing."

"Oh, no," I said. I touched his shoulder, saw my hand heading there before I knew I was moving it. "You're very, very good."

"To tell you the truth, my days here are numbered," he said. "They want somebody older in Men's. I'm too young to look like I know what I'm talking about."

"I'm the one who doesn't know what she's talking about. I don't know why I've wasted your time. You probably have better things to do," I said. I didn't mean anything by it. It seemed only what he was owed for his time, but his eyes widened and he offered me his hand. "I have an idea," he said. He led me through the islands of clothing and down an isle and we were in Women's. "A woman like you should wear something more bright," he said. We laughed. He collected a series of loud blouses as we walked to the dressing room, heaping them over his arm. Hangers fell from neck holes and he left them behind on the floor. If I'm being honest, I'll admit I was confused, out of my element. I didn't know

3

how to read the damp heat in his touch. Maybe this was the kind of naughty shopping adventure any salesman might enjoy or maybe he was a straight-up lout. The risk of guessing wrong and causing a scene in the store kept me moving right along with him. He urged me around a wall of angled mirrors and pulled the cord on the back of my neck that took down my halter tank. Then he slipped his wet hands beneath my bra and squeezed my nipples with an aggressive firmness. I stopped him at that and made the strange excuse of needing to hit the dry cleaners before they closed, as if that were all that was keeping me from giving a free lay to a stranger.

"You wanted it," he said. He gripped the swollen member in his wrinkle-free Dockers. "You'll think about this later when you get home."

I don't know how I got out of the dressing room, but I know I sat in the car and listened to the radio until I could settle my hands enough to drive and then I went home. Two weeks later, my husband Noah was on the couch making three piles of money when I came in with one of those rotisserie chickens for dinner. The first thing he said was, "What do you think you're doing?"

I said, "What do you think *you're* doing?" I thought it was a game we were playing. A little volleying before we sat down to eat.

"OK. You can try to deny it," he said.

"Deny what?"

I set my bag on the counter and turned. He folded one third of the money into his back pocket and made a show of putting the rest on the coffee table. "That's all you're getting out of me so don't ask for more," he said.

"Deny what?" I asked again.

"You're screwing around on me with some asshole who works at the J.C. Penny on State Street," he said. My head went dark and I almost lost my balance.

"I'm not screwing around," I said. I reached for the edge of the counter to steady myself and it wasn't there. "It's not what you think."

"Trace was right," he said. "You're a sneak and you're a whore."

We'd been married five years and those were the first harsh words Noah had ever used on me. I could see in his face that he was scared of doing it, a part of him feeling like he should defend me against his other, angrier parts.

"Trace is wrong," I said.

"He's not a liar. Go ahead and call him one, though. Keep insulting me."

How Noah's friend Trace had come upon the fact of this man at all was beyond me. I'd never confessed to anyone. I considered it a dark turn I'd sort out when I had the kind of quiet and distance required of such matters. And how it had become the sort of story it had become was another matter entirely. Trace had me meeting the man in bars, straddling him in the back seat of cars. When, I wondered, was I supposed to have been doing all of that?

"Have you been with him here in the house too?" said Noah. "Oh, God. It's like I'm afraid to touch anything now."

We spent too long debating Trace's trustworthiness and then Noah confessed to me that he'd cried in front of him earlier that day. "Do you know what my father said about crying in front of other men?" he asked as he left the house. I knew what his father said, what every father said about crying. It meant you were a pussy. And it meant Noah would have to bluster and blow, drive his truck all crazy in the side-yard. To do anything less would be confessing more than tears. I listened as our newly seeded grass fell victim to his Super Swamper tires and thought about how we should just pave it over because there were going to be more fights. When he came back inside, he sat me on the couch and told me he was going to kill the man from the store. "Give me his name," he said. Then he said he wasn't going to kill anybody. "The most I'll do is teach his face a lesson," he said.

"I'm telling you, I never knew his name."

"You think you can keep me from him?" he asked. "I know where he God-damn works."

"I swear on everything holy that I don't know his name," I said. It was the first time in the course of the episode that I raised my voice.

"Fine, I believe you," he said. He flicked the issue aside with his wrist. "But that's even worse. Don't you see how that's worse?"

"Noah, I never cheated on you. That's not what happened."

"Then what did happen?"

I thought about it. How to express to my husband that I was too ignorant to stop a complete stranger from trying to strip and fuck me in the dressing room of the J.C. Penny. "I don't know," I said. "But it isn't what you think. I'd never do that to you. You know I wouldn't."

Noah talked divorce while he stuffed his green army surplus duffle with clothes. At the last he railed about his quality as a husband. "I'm the type you don't find anymore," he said. "I believe in marriage like it's God. And you toss it away for this character who works in clothing? What kind of asshole works in clothing?"

At that point, I wished I knew the man's name. I would have pointed him out in the local phone book and handed over gas money from my pile on the table. *Go. Do violence. Get yourself arrested.* But he'd never given it and I'd never asked and I doubted I would have remembered even if he had. I asked Noah to stay. I reached for him and he stopped me from touching him with a slap.

"You sit on that couch and you stay," he said. "You reap what you God-damned sow." I sat there for longer than was sane. He was gone for hours and it was night and the front door was still flung open. I was obeying.

When I got up, I drank. I drank because it's what you do. People's lives blow up and they turn fish. They *need* a drink. I've never believed in the power of liquor to ameliorate the dent of sins and I've never been a drinker, never liked the feel or taste of it, but I stood up from the couch and took down as much as I could take. Ask anybody what you do when you're twenty-two years old and your husband leaves you because of some bizarre and sinister misunderstanding. In a place like Athens, where the main drag is a needy litter of bars, you see people drinking and wilding all of the time and for far less compelling reasons. You see happy college students putting their faces through plate-glass storefronts, old women in gas stations wailing in coolers. You see people passed out in sweet pairs on lawns, girls with their skirts on upsidedown and backward, suited professorial types climbing up awnings with bottles. *And now you'll see me*, I thought. *You'll see me*.

This went on for days. And then I woke to the feel of something wrong near my head—dead leaves and dirt—and had all of the low feelings from the night before come back to me before I remembered what they were about. There was a sheet of pain and just behind that, the deepest shadows of sadness. I was in the front yard and my long hair was around me like a net or a trap I'd sprung on myself. My mouth was thick with the taste of liquor and there was a bottle near my head. Across the street, the neighbors had a pair of young deer dressed out and strung up with cords, their heads flung back like they were worshiping the sky. Their chests were hollow red gashes in the fog.

Noah would have taken care of that rural grotesquerie. He would have demanded the bodies be moved somewhere around the back so I wouldn't have to deal with the sight of them, but Noah was gone and his absence pulled my throat so tight I couldn't breathe. The scene of his departure came around a corner in my mind where it had been waiting to deliver the bad news: *You're on your own now, honey.* And I knew that I had lost some time to a crisis of spirits, but I didn't know how much time or how much trouble I'd sewn.

The splintered recollection of harsh words exchanged with the neighbors—*you'll pull down those corpses or find out what I mean when I say I'm serious*—did not bode especially well. Nor did the sky's gravel-grayness that said it was early rather than late. The birds were still doing their disoriented morning chatter and I knew the school buses would be beating down the ridge in a matter of minutes. The women in the neighborhood would be tugging their children to curb and the men would be

9

coming out in their utility boots, thermoses under their arms, to head into town for work. They'd all see me there, this strange woman in the weeds, and have decisions to make. Do you talk to that woman? Is it any of your business? Does she really need your help? What would she have done for you?

In this part of town, such things generally merit at least a "Ma'am?" and even that seemed far too much for me to broker in the state I was in. Plus, the possibility that the neighbors might emerge and stage a refrain on the previous evening's theme—a poisoned debate about who has the right to come on whose property and what they're allowed to say once they get there—made my head rattle. I needed to move quickly or face the consequences of discovery. The blanket we usually kept on the couch, the one good for television watching, was at my feet. I draped it around like a cape and took stock. Skinned knees and a tear down the front of my tee-shirt, all I had on. *Bread Winner*, it said. One I got for free when we signed up for credit and used as a nightgown. At least I'd been headed for bed.

Inside the kitchen, there were signs of a historic bender. Every last bottle was emptied and on its side— even the ouzo left over from New Year's. An improvised ashtray made of the stained bowls of the sink looked like something that might happen in a bar, the sheer immensity of it. This kind of evidence, I could have predicted. I accepted this as right, as necessary. Of course I drank and smoked everything in the world. But there were other, more frightening signs. I didn't know what they meant or might suggest. Every item inside the refrigerator had been removed and placed nicely on the countertop: eggs rolled into a tidy line, trays of meat stacked like bricks in a little floodwall against the tide of condiments. The doors of the old machine hung open, the light inside was burned out, and its hum had been replaced with an irritated grind.

Alone on a shelf in the freezer sat a butter-yellow, ceramic bird. Noah had given it to me maybe three years prior. It was a gift with very little significance. He'd picked it up at a yard sale for a quarter and thought I'd like it. No special occasion commemorated, no meaning attached. Why on earth would I have put that there so deliberately? Fear came over me, the hot prickling kind that only comes when you're blindsided, caught unawares, and then there was nausea. I took to the hall, thinking I'd make it to the toilet in time to vomit, but I saw the inside of the bedroom before I could. There wasn't a stitch on the bed and in the open window the bones of a half-eaten chicken were hung in the blinds by the wings. As though the dead bird had imagined escape. As though it had meant to fly away to safety.

In the end, I couldn't stay in the house, which meant I had to make myself presentable enough to go out. The mess in the bathroom simplified some matters. There was nothing to be done with my looks. All of my makeup, every tube of lipstick, every tiny tub of color, had been gutted in the sink. My hairbrushes and toothbrush were in the toilet. Noah's spare razors stood upright like always in the medicine cabinet and his green hair gel was the only bottle left on any shelf. I'd stayed away from his items and gone selectively for the items that were explicitly mine or shared, but understood generally as mine. I reasoned that I must have wanted to punish myself pretty badly for trying to be pretty. That, at least, I could understand.

I pulled on a high-necked sweater and some jeans and I went to Trace's house. I wanted to know how he'd come to know about the man at Penny's and I wanted him to see the mess I was in. To my way of thinking, it was his mess too. We had a sometimes sour history, Trace and I. Next to me he was the closest person to Noah and I guessed that made him feel he had a right to test me. He'd once taken my knee into his hands and brought it to his mouth as though to bite it, an awkward maneuver in the back of a parked car; he'd once suggested my breasts were almost above average for Ohio; and he'd once invited me to his trailer in the Plains for a round of *Girltalk*, a board game he claimed was fun for the whole family. On the occasion of Noah's birthday one year, he told me I was as pretty as a porkchop and touched my hair. Not once had I ever ratted out Trace for being a handsy asshole, but maybe I would have if I'd known he would call me a whore.

There were three dogs chained to his deck—he called them his hillbilly doorbell—and they all went mad as I approached. He answered the door with his shirt off and his belt undone. His hair stood high on his head. "You're here," he said. "I expected you'd call."

"I'm angry," I said.

"At me?"

He took a long breath and rubbed his eyes with the heels of his palms. "You can come in," he said and waved me in through the screen door. He walked to a couch so covered in dog hair it seemed alive and pulled a shirt from between two cushions.

"You aren't denying it," he said. "I respect that, but you shouldn't have done it. It was the wrong thing to do to a man like Noah. Let's face it, the guy's high strung."

I wanted to sit somewhere and stop my hands from shaking in my hangover, but there was nowhere but the couch and Trace was standing in front of it, facing me as though to tell me with his body, *let's keep this brief, OK?* I moved to the wall beside the television and leaned against it to avoid a wave of nausea.

"Wait," he said. "You're physically sick. I thought you were just emotional."

"It's none of your business."

"You need water. Come into the kitchen."

I followed him into a dark room that smelled of food left out and sat at a table while he filled a glass from the tap. He observed me from the sink.

"I don't know if you've seen your face but it's like death woke up in there. I'm not a professional, but I know a hangover when I see one."

"You had no right telling Noah anything. You have no idea what happened and it's none of your concern anyway."

Trace drank from the glass and then refilled it for me. It was probably the only glass he owned, so it was hard to fault him for manners. While I drank his coppery, lukewarm tap water, he made a chant of a word. "Girl," he said. "Girl, girl, girl, girl, girl."

"What?"

"You are in trouble."

"What do you know about it?"

"I'll tell you what I know. How many girls in town have a name like yours?"

I should pause here to acknowledge that I have the most redneck name in the history of redneck names. Sister. My mother named me after her aunt Sissy, who was not technically a Sister, but rather a Cecile, who was also a sister to her mother, and thus *Cece* became *Sissy*. My mother was seventeen when she had me, so I could forgive her for this mistake, though I'd been paying for it, paying for it, paying for it, for all of my years on the planet.

"There's only one of me in Athens," I said.

"And you're married to Noah," he said. "That prick you slept with works at the mall where I work janitorial Tuesdays and Thursdays. He's locking up and he says to me, 'You ever done it with a Sister?' and right then I know what he's talking about. He's making a joke on your name. I say, 'No way, what's she look like?' because I'm giving everybody a chance. I'm hoping it isn't you even though I already know it's you. And then he describes your hair, says it's so long you could make a dress out of it, says he's seen you in nothing but that dress right there in the store. And then I don't know what to do so I take his legs out from under him and kick him while he's down on the floor."

"That was it?" I said. "I hope you lost your job."

"I lost my job *and* he's pressing charges. That's how Noah knows about you and this guy. Because he was still over here yesterday when the cops came by. They had the whole story written out on paper for me to verify or deny. So don't accuse me of sticking my nose in where it doesn't belong. I'm up to my eyeballs in this."

"You've known me for how many years?" I pressed my palms into the table and did my best to look Trace in the eye.

"I don't know," he said. "Sevenish, I guess."

"And you believe this person when he says he slept with me without questioning it? Because he knew my name?"

He shrugged, evaded my glare. "Are you saying it didn't happen?"

"The guy tried to get a look at my tits in a dressing room, OK? That's all."

"That's your version of events."

The inside of the kitchen became a dark pair of spinning plates, one above me and one below. In the middle of all this movement, I saw Trace lean his face in near mine. His mouth was moving, his lips. "I can't talk to you," I said. He picked me up by my armpits and carried me to the couch, where he tried to talk to me again. And then he went out the front and stomped around on the porch. I smelled his cigarette burning and it took me to Noah, of the light scent of tobacco in his shirts and jeans, of the old trick he played, tossing a cigarette out of a soft pack and into his waiting mouth. The thought of him made me cry and then cry even harder when I couldn't stop, when there was nothing to be done but sit on Trace's disgusting couch and weep like a child. *This is where I am,* I thought. *This is the point at which I have arrived.*

With a cigarette still burning in his mouth, Trace lifted me over his shoulder like a jumbo sack of flour. Like a thing. My head was at his middle near his belt-line and my hair dragged on the ground. He got me into my truck on the passenger side and buckled me in. I knew what he was thinking. I was a disease now, one spread by touch. He had to get me away from his house or risk infection, accusation.

"Where are your keys?" he asked. "I'm not going in your pockets."

I heard him, but I couldn't will my body to move. I didn't know where the keys were. Tears came down my face in a solid stream, turning the orange of my sweater something like red.

"You had a purse. You probably had a purse," he said. He moved my legs to the side and looked beneath my feet, pulled the center console down and looked inside that. He ran back into the house and then came out again with his hands in his hair and his shirt half untucked. The dogs cried for him every time he passed and he touched their heads, talking to himself. He made the last trip back to the truck slowly. He pulled himself into the driver's seat and leaned his head back to the glass of the cab.

"I know you can't really hear me because you're in some sort of dissociative state or whatever," he said. "But I need to tell you that I have to go into your pockets to get your keys. I'm not trying to pull anything on you, I just need to get in there to look."

He blew hard out of his nose and took one more look in the console, behind each of the sun visors. "OK," he said. He took me by the hips and turned me towards him. My thighs locked, the muscles inside iron solid, and there they were, hanging there. Five silver keys, one gold, and a bottle opener from Key West that said *Southernmost Point* touching my knee.

"Ignition," I said. It came out of me in a yelp, the bark of a tiny dog. "Look in the damn ignition."

Back at my devastated house, Trace hunted for the phone so he could call the hospital. "Why didn't you tell me this was the deal?" he asked. "I thought you were only there to pull my eyes out. I didn't realize you needed help." He moved around the place, righting pictures on the wall, filling the bin with trash from the floor while he searched. "You're clearly unwell." He sat me in the recliner and tucked the television blanket around me. Then he collected my hands in my lap and brushed the wet off my face with his sleeve. "Did you take any pills?"

"I'm fine," I said. "You don't need to call the hospital. They'll only tell you what I've been telling you, which is that I was upset and I got drunk."

"Give me the phone," he said. "I don't believe it."

"I guess I'm not surprised. You don't seem to believe a word I say," I said. I walked unsteadily to the guest bedroom and shoved the cordless phone deeper into the hamper where I remembered burying it the night before. Bits and flecks of memories arrived in my head as I passed through the hall: the hour I'd spent carefully draining each bottle of nail polish down the walls, the collage I'd constructed of wedding photos, floral wire, and sliced lunch meat. Trace was waiting for me in the living room, hands hipped, when I came back. Beneath his right shoe was a cheaply framed picture of Jesus petting a lamb. I remembered exhuming it from Noah's trunk of treasured childhood possessions. And then I remembered what I'd done with his high school football uniform.

"Did Noah do this?" he asked. "You don't have to tell me if he did. I don't think I want to know about it." He pushed down a cushion on the couch and saw the series of steak knives, stabbed to the hilt. "No, I do want to know about it," he said. "I think I need to hear it."

"We can sit in the kitchen," I said.

"I was in there and there's food stacked in a disturbing way. You don't want to go in there." I could hear in his voice that the stacks of food frightened him and that made me feel even worse about it. What did it mean that I'd done this to my own house?

"The bedroom is worse," I said.

"I didn't get a good look."

"There's meat hung in the window. It made me sick and I couldn't get it down."

"I'll take care of it," he said and stalked off. There was the sound of the metal blinds folding and colliding and then a thud I imagined was the bird finally taking flight outside. "It's OK to come in now," he said. "This room doesn't seem to be as bad as the rest."

He had the bedclothes thrown across the bed so I could sit in the middle, away from the chocolate milk stains down the side. He took up a position against the wall in the corner nearest the closet. I worried he'd turn his head and see the scarecrows I'd constructed out of our clothes. They were stuffed with grass and leaves from the compost and their faces were made of paper plates, open holes for eyes.

"I don't understand what's happening here," he said. "There's vomit in the hall. There's about a million cigarettes burned straight down to the filter in the sink. The yellow bird in the kitchen. I don't know what to think about the bird in there. I want to know what all this means, but I don't want to know."

"I was drinking," I said. I leaned into the head-board and heard dry leaves in my hair give. It sounded as though there was a whole tree of them in there, a crisp fall bonnet.

"You don't drink," he said. "You're, like, the good ship lollipop. I've never seen you finish a beer."

"Well, I drank a lot, Trace," I said. Loud. "Alright?"

"You couldn't have done all that. That's the work of a mob."

"I must have. I did."

"Why would you do that? Why *that*?" He stuck his fingers in the blinds and shook them.

"I did not sleep with that man," I said. "He groped me and I was too ashamed to tell it."

A long spell of silence passed between us, the only sounds the chimes on all the neighborhood porches making their hollow tune like a song descending in wa-ter, and distant wheels turning gravel. It was a silence in which I saw myself, face ablaze with alcohol, turning over the house with a plow of anger. I saw myself taking that yellow bird in my hands with an intent as criminally random as frost and Trace saw the same. I could see it in his face, which was still and sad. His Adam's apple sunk like he was swallowing a fist.

"You believe me," I said.

"Yes."

"He came onto me and I didn't handle it well. That's all. He unfastened my blouse before I knew what was happening. Does that make me a whore?"

"I said I believe you. I don't need the details." He slid down the wall like there was a chair waiting to catch him, a tiny invisible seat.

"And then I was trapped because I did something wrong but it wasn't the wrong thing you two thought it was and I didn't know what to do and I guess I lost my mind."

"I get it, I get it."

"I'm not very experienced with men. I met Noah when I was a teenager. You know what happened then. We had sex twice and then we got married."

"I'm not sure I know what we're getting into here," he said. He stood up slowly and raked down his jeans in the knees. "I don't think I want to be in this conversation." With hands so light and cautious that he barely touched me, he laid me back in the bed and crossed my hands over my chest. I didn't realize I was scared until he spoke. "What do you want to do?" he asked.

"I have to sleep," I said. I held myself in my arms.

"Then sleep," he said. He straightened himself and leaned into the wall. "I'm not leaving this place until I know it's safe."

"Fine. Suit yourself."

I thought about my first date with Noah. Trace had been there, as had another boy whose name I couldn't remember. We'd gone out in a group—three guys and three girls—and I knew as soon as I saw him that Noah would be mine. My gaze had never wavered since then. Not once. We had one of those marriages that happened in other, distant generations. He went to work at the guitar plant at 8 a.m. and I had dinner steaming on the table at 5 p.m. I put a cold beer in his hand and there were five more just like it in the fridge. Sometimes he'd take me into a swoop kiss. I'd be nearly floor-side and the next moment my hands would be back in the dishwater and scrubbing. I was in the kind of marriage so safe people thought it was boring—and they were right.

Nobody ever said it would last. One lunch at the university cafeteria where my mother worked had decided my fate. She told me I was headed for tragedy and I shot her a shattering look over my bowl of chili. "Your father is talking about putting a bullet in this boy," she said. "Or there's the courts. You're underaged, so it's rape." We had our wedding reception in that same cafeteria, dorm kids wandering through in their pajama pants, demanding to be fed. There were toasts about young love, how often it was fleeting. *Here's hoping*, was the joke. And the frequent speculation I was knocked up and needling Noah into the old right thing, which was

23

the new wrong thing. At the end of the night we got into my father's ancient Buick and we pulled off together. Our loved ones imagined us driving that old boat slow and straight into disaster. At the horizon we'd find the sky had fallen off and we'd know no better than to keep on driving.

As far as cheating, it had never occurred to me. Noah was the only man I'd ever been with. He was it. I believed we'd been made for each other. God set us down in the same small town so that we wouldn't have any trouble figuring it out. As for him, he always said he wasn't the type to notice anybody noticing him. He said the idea of an affair was ridiculous to him. More than once, he'd talked about how that would never, ever happen. He saw it all the time at work and was disgusted by it. "These people have no shame," he'd once said. "They do it in supply closets with their wedding rings on."

"I can't even believe that," I'd said.

"Believe it," he'd said. "That's the world and we're living in it."

I wondered what would happen if I went back in time and found myself on that first date again. Would I choose Noah? Would he choose me? Who were we if we weren't Sister-and-Noah, equal parts of the same dopey, sing-songy phrase? I felt like a broken home— the human picture of the idea.

The sky was sweetheart pink when I woke and it filled the room with a damp heat that clung to the detached sheets. There was a dark spot in the hall, where a good deal of scrubbing had gone on. The kitchen showed signs of work. All the food was gone and the fridge was pulled away from the wall. I followed the scent of a cigarette burning and half expected to find Noah on the porch where Trace sat. There was a black bag of trash at his feet and seven more bags at the end of the drive. He fumbled with his cigarette, trying to stand and turn at the same time. "Scared me a little," he said.

"You didn't have to clean all that up," I said.

He slid over on the stoop and made room for me. It was cooler outside. There was a nip in the air. "I feel bad," he said. He stirred the bag with his feet. "There is a way of looking at all of this that makes it seem like it's my fault your marriage is all screwed up."

"How screwed up is it?" I asked.

"Well," he said. His eyebrows lifted and his eyes went down. "We'll get to that."

I imagined the point at which we'd *get to that* and it was not especially welcome. The worst I could imagine was Noah telling his folks I'd cheated. I hated to think of their judgment, of him sleeping on their couch, the dogs pestering him for attention, and them thinking he didn't deserve such low treatment. Once he told his parents, they'd tell mine and then it would be everywhere that I'd been unfaithful. No matter what kind of explaining I did, there would always be suspicion. Noah would always be a wronged man. That was the way of the small town.

Trace and I sat and both stared at the spotted pelts of the deer. They had been scraped and were now curing.

"That's disgusting," I said, pointed.

He took a long time thinking and then said, "It's not even deer season. It's fox and grey squirrel season. I heard it on the radio. 'Looks like a bad year for grey squirrel. Low acorn production.'"

"Acorn production?"

"I'm not even kidding. Swear it to God." He drew a cross of smoke in the air. "I tune in during hunting season so I can hear about the jackasses falling out of their stands and shooting each other. 'Seven killed by heart attacks in woods today. Animals seven, people none.'"

"You tune in regular?"

"I know people who have died. I've worked with them. Normal people every other kind of way, but then they shoot themselves leaning a rifle against a tree."

"Those are baby deer," I said. "I don't care what season it is."

I told him about the confrontation I'd had with the neighbors, the eighteen-year-old who'd answered his door with a plastic bottle full of tobacco-browned spit and told me I could fuck myself if I thought he was taking down those deer. "My kill, my property," he'd said. "You go back in your house and bake bread or whatever you do all day."

Trace and I walked over there without talking about it. There were lights on in the house, blue din of a television coming through the blinds. A game show, crowds cooing a prize and the low sound of male voices. Methodical as paid workers, Trace and I took down the deer. We set them in a grass grove about a mile up the ridge with the kind of respect you reserve for your fallen. Like little soldiers they were, their heads tucked into each other's fallen chests.

I made dinner because it's what you do when you're hungry and your life has exploded. It's as natural as breathing. You take what there is to eat and you eat it. There was bread in the box that had survived the night and canned soup. Tomato, the worst kind. A soup so straight it might as well be medicine you're spoonfulling into your stupid mouth. I told Trace as much at the table and then he told me about his mother, how she'd pour generics and government-issues into old brand-name bottles she'd used over and over because there might be company. How she'd gone into a rage when a cousin threw a Heinz bottle into the trash, breaking it. And then he looked like he might be sick. He let his spoon fall deep into the soup, too far to avoid a mess getting it out. "I know where Noah is," he said.

There was a rush in my ears like my heart was heaving itself overboard, like it was turning itself over to the sea. "Tell me," I said and then regretted it.

"You're not going to want to hear this."

"He's with his parents, right? Did he tell them what happened, what he thought happened?"

He closed his eyes. "I don't think you have to worry about him telling," he said.

"Good," I said. "At least there's that, right?" I expected my relief to find its match in Trace's face, but he was looking at the ceiling.

"Jesus Christ," he said. "I could kill myself right now. There's a woman Noah knows at work. Somebody he's known a long time and always thought about. Nothing ever went on between them, but he's always known it could."

"What about her? He told her?"

"He's with her."

I didn't get it at first, imagining a spare bedroom. "If he's staying there, you could call him," I said. "Tell him the truth."

Trace shook his head. "I know where he is, but I don't know where that is. And besides. He's *with* her with her."

I leaned back in my chair and remembered a conversation Noah and I had had about a woman where he worked who colored her hair plum and wore a spiked silver bolt through her tongue. *I always thought people like that were assholes trying to piss off their parents, but she's OK,* he'd said. *We actually relate.* I pictured them in his car after work, a mix she'd made playing on headphones split between them. I knew she liked music.

"You mean they're together."

"Yes," he said. "That's what I'm telling you."

"Is her name Amelia? She likes to be called Mel by her friends. Is that what you call her?"

"Yes. That's what we call her."

I could hardly believe the two of them, Noah and Trace. They'd had conversations about this woman. That was clear. Perhaps they'd imagined what she'd be like in bed, plotted it out. And the first chance he gets to leave our bed, the first excuse, Noah takes it. And Trace supports him, giving him the OK, the all clear, based on some story he's heard in the mall.

"He said I'd hear from him in a day or two when he figured things out," he said.

"I don't want to know any more about it." Bile rose in my throat, a rank chemical anger I didn't know I could have for my husband or anyone.

"I'll tell him I was wrong. I'll explain everything and then he'll be back."

"It's too late. It's over."

"He'll be back. You two are the real deal. No doubt about it."

First, my head was a giant ball of lead. It was headed for the floor. Then the rest of my body, also leadened, wanted to follow. *The real deal.* Trace caught me before I could fall. "You're not going to go crazy again, are you?" he asked. "Can you hear me?"

I slapped his hands from my shoulders and wiped my eyes with my sleeve. "I can hear you," I said.

"What do you want? Do you want to lay down again? Do you want something to drink? Some juice?"

"I'm not crazy," I said. "And you don't have to talk to me like I'm a kid. You just told me my husband is with another woman. That has effects on a person."

"I get it, I get it."

"You're all assholes and you're all the same."

"Who?" he asked. "Men?"

I nodded. "Are you surprised that's news to me?"

"A little, to be honest. I guess I thought that was clear to anyone living."

I put my head between my knees and watched my tears hit the linoleum. There were tiny geese, their wings spread in patterned V's in the floor and my crying on them was just how I'd imagined rain happened as a child. Some greater, larger being weeping down on us from above. Every surface in the house seemed suddenly this way, wet with my grief which spread vertically, horizontally. There were no rules to its movement, nothing stopping it or directing it.

"Get me to the bathroom," I said.

I sat on the bathroom floor for an hour before it finally came to me: I'd destroyed my home because there was nowhere else for me to go. I wanted it cashed. Trace was right on the other side of the door. I didn't have to see him there to know; I could feel him there, hesitating. I reached up and turned the knob. "Can we go to your house?" I asked.

"Let's take that option off the table right now."

I stood up and yanked my sweater down where it had flipped up like a fat lip in the front. "I thought we had a deal. I thought you understood me."

"I can take you anywhere else but there."

"Screw it," I said. "Do whatever you want. I can take care of myself."

I walked around the house and collected what I could. The stack of comforters in the hall closet we kept for guests. One pillow—mine that smelled of my hair. A

31

pair of sweats and old gym shoes. I found my purse beneath the sink with a half-full bottle of water inside. A treat I'd been saving for myself, apparently. Trace watched me make three trips to the truck. He stood in the kitchen window and saw me flinging comforters and shoes into the bed. And then he saw me climbing into the bed. I sat and organized the bedding around me and then I straightbacked it down. I must have seemed to disappear to him, as though into a self-dug pickup grave. He gave it a few minutes, probably paced around, kicking at things. When he finally came out of the house, he had anger in his walk. Seven quick steps and he was there, knocking at the side paneling. "You can't stay out here," he said.

"Why not?"

"It isn't safe."

"What else do you want me to do?"

I let him stand there in the cold, considering, his breath in the air the only sign of him I could see. I expected he'd pace awhile, maybe curse at me. *If some animal comes along after the smell of those deer and finds you, don't blame me*, he'd say. *Don't say I didn't warn you if those punks down the ridge show up and decide to have some fun.* Instead, he climbed directly into the bed with me. He slid me over and pulled the double layer of comforters over us both. I expected he'd sleep then, his body as distant as possible from me, arranged at an angle that couldn't be construed as intimate. But he pulled me toward him. "Come here," he said. "You'll freeze." He curved me into the larger hook of himself and put my hands together inside of his own, as though I were a child and he was teaching me how to hold still, how to urge myself into a more true calm. We slept for a time. I don't know how long, though I can say that the moon moved from one corner of our rectangle of sky to another. He woke when I stirred and he cleared his throat. I could see light reflecting in his eyes and feel the heat of his mouth on mine as he opened it to yawn. We were that close. He seemed to notice this and pulled back, withdrawing his spine and his warmth along with it.

"You're OK," I said.

He stopped moving, abrupt like he'd been caught. His breathing quickened, his heart beat a tight rhythm, his feet and hands were clenched in tense angles. He didn't know what to do. It was a window, I realized. And not the kind you see through. Like black glass, you see only your own dark reflection in it. I took Trace's face and turned his mouth into mine. There was resistance like a caught door and then none. Aches of sounds in the back of his throat, light as filament. We were undressed by the time those sounds became words. "This shouldn't be happening," he said. "It isn't right." He held my hands, but I didn't stop. I wouldn't. September's brightest stars were above us, a triangle without

33

the lines, and I fucked that man like he'd never been fucked before.

I could have guessed Trace would be gone when I woke, but I was still surprised to find myself alone. I spent the afternoon in the truck, leaving only to use the bathroom. I heard the occasional car pass and wondered: who was in it, where were they going? There were little bits of gravel in the truck bed. I tossed them up and let them land on me, on my face. Why not? When I was too hungry to think, I moved inside. I ate bread on the couch and sat on the floor. And this was how my day passed.

Another day passed and there was a note stuffed into the handle of the screen door. I spent an hour deciding whom I wished to be the author. Trace or Noah. Now or later. But it was only the neighbors, upset about their missing deer. *We know it was you,* it said. *Consider yourselves warned.* I'd taken to sitting in the yard, preferring it to the house, a move the neighbors probably considered oddly confrontational. I watched the neighborhood happen around me from my pink plastic yard chair, the kids ticking off to school, the birds on the humming line. Slowly, very slowly, I was moving myself. I'd made it to the de-bloomed forsythia leaning near the edge of the drive. The sun came out from behind the peak of the roof there and you could sit without a coat and watch for the next thing coming down the road. Eventually, Trace came and he had some news. He pulled in slow and came out of his car even slower.

"What's the story?" I asked.

"Noah," he said. He tapped at the bill of his hat and then balled his fists into the pockets of his jeans. "He came over last night around midnight."

"What's he going to do?" I sat up in my chair.

"He wants to come home."

"Did you tell him?"

"I told him everything I could, which I guess is about half of the whole." His face revealed only the fact that the sun was in his eyes, but his feet fooling in the gravel said he was all nerves and there was more that must pass between us. "I don't know what to say," he said.

"You don't have to worry about me telling him," I said. "I never would. I swear."

He laughed. A quick sound that had the weight of a heavy thought to it. "I'm not too worried about that," he said. He spun on his heel and laughed. As he walked away, he ran his hand along the bed of my truck, a soft touch, one with little contact to it. At the tailgate, he paused, gripping the corner joints. "You'll take care of yourself, Sister," he said, "you're stronger than you think you are." And then he was gone, his wheels turning up a white wall of gravel dust that lingered when the sound of him was long gone. I knew he wouldn't dare come back. By some standards, maybe even his own, he'd done the worst you could do. He slept with his best friend's wife. But he'd only done it because I'd asked him to.

Somehow, in the way the sun landed fully on my back that afternoon, I knew Noah would be rolling up the drive soon. He'd see me sitting in my chair and he'd know I'd been waiting for him. He'd see his wife and I'd see my husband, and the world would turn as it always had, only with a little more spin now to the throw. It would take him a while, but he'd get there. He'd come around.

II.

I came into the kitchen and said tights or hose. "Pants," said my son. It was Christmas and we were going to see his father Trace, a nice man who was not my husband. My husband Noah, also a nice man, would meanwhile be sitting at home alone on Christmas, waiting for his wife and the son he'd raised since birth to return to him. This was the source of a good deal of awkwardness for all of us, but especially Will. He was fourteen and so sensitive he could seem disturbed. He started when touched, words seemed to bruise the air around him. He had a perilous attachment to a dark, hooded sweatshirt, one large enough to conceal him completely from head to knees. Like a chess piece, he slid silently across rooms, his pointy hood sometimes bent high at the tip, a tiny cartoonish angle.

Will and I were in a constant state of negotiation over what he called *The Rules of Mom*. If I wanted to control the way he looked, I couldn't control the way he ate. If I wanted straight A's, I had to give up on sports. I was allowed access to his room, provided he had access to ours—there was a larger television in there and he liked to sprawl out on the king-sized bed, his blinking the only thing happening on his face. Today the issue was attitude. I wanted him to seem happy, even if he was faking. In exchange, we were spending only two hours with Trace. One hour for dinner, one for gifts, and then we were back on the road to Athens. He wanted to be home early enough to get a few good hours of online gaming in.

I had one leg in solid black tights and the other was bare. "Come on," I said. "I can't change the whole outfit now."

"What does it matter what you look like? You're married," he said.

"Watch it," I said. He liked to bait me in this way, remind me of my age, my irrelevance. "I have it in my power to spend Christmas night in Lancaster. We have a hotel reservation."

"Fine," he said. "Tights. But those are stupid. You should do the skin-colored ones."

"Thank you. Was that so hard?"

His face told me that it was immensely, impossibly hard. He flattened it into a kind of wall and an imperiousness drifted into his eyes. In my sock and hose drawer there were about a dozen pairs of neutral tights, all of them with some deformity or flaw. Some of them were missing entire legs. I'd match opposites together and hope the subtle differences in shade were undetectable. Pulling the right pair from the heap was like performing a complicated surgical procedure. I had the whole dresser drawer tossed out on the floor and was running my hand up the legs of each frantically when Will and Noah came into the bedroom. They were both there to see what was taking me so long.

"Guys," I said. "I'm in a crisis here."

"What's the big deal?" said Noah.

"The black ones are good," said Will. "They're more regal. Elegant."

"Really? I was afraid they were dowdy," I said.

"They're fine," said Will. "Don't worry."

"I was planning on wearing the other ones tonight anyway," said Noah. "Once I'm all alone." He took Will's head under his arm and they walked themselves out of the room like a two-headed creature. When I arrived downstairs in the black tights, they applauded me. "Bravo," they said. "Well done." They'd obviously planned.

"Now get out of here," said Noah. "The sooner you leave, the sooner you're back." He gave Will a hang-in-there pat on the back and fed us into the car.

Although Trace had lived in Lancaster for most of Will's life, a forty-five-minute haul up Route 33, he'd been a good father to him. He'd never missed an important event, even when he'd started a new family of his own and had twin daughters to wrangle. The girls were infatuated with Will like he was some dark god of a teenaged filament. And Will made a game of pretending not to like them. He'd frown terribly, stomp and storm. Then he'd show up in their playroom, wearing a princess crown and a pink feather-boa. They divined in him, the twins. They wanted him to carry them into constellations of coolness and detachedness. For her part, Trace's wife Kara was a model of coolness for Will. She'd been an adjunct art professor before she had the twins and she knew about things like music.

But Will had always been fiercely loyal to Noah, a man he also called his father, sometimes with the word *true* attached. He had trouble with the fact that unlike most of his friends with more than one father, his mother had never been divorced. This meant that his mother had cheated, something that had only really dawned on him recently—at about the same time sex hit him as a dirty concept with some hot particulars to it. We'd explained the events leading up to his conception, probably badly, as a dark but wonderful turn of events. He'd come out of the mix somehow and that was a gift we'd never expected. Like God coming straight down and filling your pockets with diamonds, your hands full of gold, when what you deserve is less than the dust of coal. Will had the idea that a full-on acceptance of Trace would seem like a betrayal of Noah, for whom his love had always been of a fanatical variety. He'd willingly die for Noah, if prompted, something he'd confessed at the age of seven after watching a PBS special on organ transplants.

"If you needed all of my organs to survive, I'd give them to you," he'd said to Noah, his little hands over the kidneys in his back.

"But that would mean you'd die," said Noah.

"I know."

"But don't you know that if you died, it would kill me?"

"I know."

"Where does that leave us?"

Will had embraced Noah at the knees then, crying and pretending not to. The conversation disturbed me. I banned all medical documentaries. In exchange, I had to forgive a carving incident with an arrowhead. *I love Dad*, carved into the arms of my grandmother's antique rocking chair. *I love Dad, I love Dad, I love Dad* running down the curving polished boughs like ticker tape. *The Rules of Mom* weren't always fair.

The drive to Lancaster was not a bad one, but we'd done it too many times. There was nothing new to see.

There was the giant wooden cross perched in the hills of Nelsonville. We used to imagine the size of the Jesus that would be attached to it, his head like a semi tire. The boot on top of Rocky Boots, a few sizes too big for our Jesus. We didn't acknowledge these landmarks now. They were reminders of our fatigue. We both felt like we were getting too old for this. "Wouldn't it be nice if they moved closer?" I asked.

"No kidding," said Will, then reconsidered. "Wait, no way. I take that back."

"I guess you're right," I said. "Then they'd want us sitting for the girls all the time."

"They're animals," he said.

"You love them."

"No, I don't. I think they're insane. They used to eat each other's snot until I told them it was wrong."

"They were toddlers."

"Why couldn't Kara tell them? She's the mother."

"She's busy. Mothers get busy. Besides, what's the big deal? It's not like snot's poisonous. It's not like they were eating asbestos."

"It's disgusting."

"You used to eat the dog's food."

"Different. Way different. If somebody was trapped and all he had was dog food, he'd eat it and he'd be OK."

"You were always down on the floor, around the corner, swiping little pellets of dog food, one at a time from the bowl. We'd catch you with it in your mouth and have to wash it out. I'll never know what the attraction was. Maybe you wanted to be a puppy."

"Mom."

"Do you know what they make dog food out of? Horses. That's where old horses go. That and glue."

"Stop the talking, Mom."

About ten minutes out from Lancaster, I started feeling the familiar falling away of my sense of ease. A faint movement at first and then a collapse like a sand cliff disappearing into a churn of water. Trace was a generally positive force in our lives, but also a fierce complication, blurring our lines of loyalty. If Noah had consented to come on these trips, I might have felt less awkward about making them. But then on the rare occasions when he did come, it was a decision we all regretted. He sulked in chairs. He criticized window treatments. He once called Kara a flake. "Fucking flake," he'd said to nobody, to everybody. Downed his wine in one draft and set his empty jelly jar in the center of the mantelpiece, as if to say that was what passed for elegance in Trace's house. "I didn't mean you," he said to Kara, though it was clear that he did. She was standing on a chair, doing scenes of the nativity in a rap for the kids, a white wad of cotton held to her chin like the beard of a wise man. "Of course not," she said. "I don't know why you'd call your son's stepmother a fucking flake on Christmas Day in front of the children."

And so Will and I drove to Lancaster without Noah, sometimes staying for a weekend, sometimes only an afternoon, knowing that Noah was sitting at home alone, doing what he did when he was alone, which was to wait impatiently until we were back. We never arrived at the other end to find Trace had been doing a great deal of waiting impatiently for us, but he did always seem happy to see us. There was a diner Will loved as a child only because it was next to the shoe store where they'd pretend to ex-ray your feet for a dollar, something about sizing the bones in the shoes themselves for a truly accurate fit. Even if he didn't need shoes, or want them, Will wanted to see that machine. He'd select the diner on the off chance we'd wander over to the shoes. Trace had asked us to meet there because Kara had her entire family at the house. He said he wanted an hour alone with his son before he had to contend with the populace. I was surprised the diner was open on Christmas, but I could see the waitresses skimming by through a window sprayed with fake ice. Trace was at the corner booth, where he said he'd be, waving with both hands and then straightening his Santa hat.

"Does he have to wear that?" asked Will.

"Every year," I said. "It's called tradition."

"It's called repetition."

Inside, the diner smelled of gravy and turkey burgers, oils crisping edges, and vanilla sugar on pies. Trace hugged Will, who loosened in his arms like a dead fish.

"Sister," said Trace. He patted the shoulder of my suit jacket. This was how our contact with each other went: so light as to be disturbing. Sometimes I wanted to embrace him, see what would happen. Would his eyes turn red? Would the sky tip out of place?

"Whatever you want on the menu," said Trace. "It's Christmas."

"Anything?" asked Will.

"Careful," I said. "This one has tricks up his sleeves." I shook Will's arm by the sleeve as he retreated into the hood of his sweatshirt. He looped the hood's cords around his hand and put the ends in his mouth.

"How was the drive?" asked Trace.

We both waited for Will to reply and then gave up on him. "Same as always," I said. "A little traffic once we hit the malls."

"It's good of you to come on Christmas," he said. "Are you sure you aren't spending the night?"

I felt Will's legs go tense beside me. He nudged me with his knee, willing me to decline the offer. "We've got

45

an early breakfast with Noah's side of the family tomorrow," I said. "Otherwise we'd be set up in the Radisson on you, watching pay-per-view all night long."

"Actually," said Trace, "that works out better anyhow."

Will relaxed in his end of the booth. I felt his feet dancing beneath the table. He loved it when I lied, got a real kick out of it. The waitress came and Will ordered his little heart's desire: a chocolate shake, a slice of pumpkin pie, and a Coke. By the time Trace and I had ordered, he was already eating sugar out the white packets at the table, tilting his head back into his hood and downing them like shots.

"Too much sugar will ruin your skin," said Trace.

"That's what dad says," said Will.

I waited for Trace to say, *I'm your dad too*, and hold up two fingers, the joke he usually made when this kind of awkwardness arose. *What I say may not go, but it kind of matters*. But his head went down and he fiddled with the silverware. Near the end of the meal, he confessed he had something to tell us. "A sort of an announcement," he said. "It's good news and bad news at the same time."

I ran through the list in my head, possible disasters that could be construed as miracles: conjoined twins, job relocations to destitute nations, eye-opening diseases.

"The bad part is that Kara and I have decided to separate," he said.

My hands went to my throat, the strained tendons there. "I'm so sorry," I said. I had no idea there was any trouble. They'd always seemed so happy. They had a TimeShare in the Hocking Hills. I wondered, oddly, what they would do with that if they divorced. Who would get it? And then I remembered they'd sold it for peanuts when the economy dipped. I told him I felt like crying and Trace settled me with a shake of his head.

"Long time coming," he said. "Not worth crying about. The good part is that I'll be moving closer to town for a while, at least until we get things figured out. I have a place in the county."

"Oh," my son and I said, "Oh, oh."

"I thought, if you're OK with it, we might all go over there on your way home after the Christmas party. I've got a tree up and there are presents under it for you. It would really mean something to me if you were the first people to visit me there on my own. The girls have been there, but nobody else. Call it a test drive or a maiden voyage."

"I don't know," I said. "Noah," I started, and then didn't know what to say. What could I say? *Noah wouldn't like that.* I felt for Will's knees under the table, some sign in his bones I should continue with a lie.

"We're OK with it," he said.

"Great," said Trace. "We'll do an hour for dinner, an hour at my new place and then you can head home. Does that sound OK with you, Sister?"

I took Will's fork and ate three bites of his pie without asking. One straight after the next, without much pause to swallow between. If Will had been thinking straight, he'd have said something. *Hungry, mom? Get your own slice.* He'd have foamed indignant.

"Is that OK with you, Mom?"

"Yes, of course," I said. "Whatever you want. It's Christmas."

We spent the agreed-upon hour at the house with Kara and her family, Will letting the twins open his presents for him and then sinking into the couch with the remote control and a candycane, while the adults loitered in the kitchen, talking politics, weather. Trace and Kara were cordial, but strained. She squeezed my hand in the hallway as we left. "We're still family," she said. "I want you to know that."

"We'll talk soon," I said, already dreading the conversation. How would we manage the arrangements? Would my son see his sisters at Kara's house or Trace's? Would he see them at all?

"I'd like that," she said.

Rather than bothering with directions, we agreed to follow Trace's car to his rental. The house was *modest*, which is what you'd say if the living you were making were *decent*. To a college kid, it'd be a palace and probably had been. There were Greek letters carved into the doorframe. It reminded me of the first place Noah and I had owned. It wasn't a trailer, but it was boxy like one. Rusted siding and a deck that leaned down like a weekend project gone drunk. There was indeed a Christmas tree, one of those ancient deals made of goose feathers and a wooden dowel.

"Where'd you scrounge that up?" I asked.

"They're all the rage," said Trace. "They display ornaments more prominently than the new artificial trees."

It wasn't the kind of thing Trace would say, would know. *All the rage*. And, sadly, there wasn't an ornament on the tree save the paper angel at the top whose crown may have been fashioned out of duct tape. Her head was definitely a bottle cap.

"Are you reading that out of a decorating magazine?" I asked.

"Kara," he said. "We found it in the basement when we were sorting through junk. She wanted it, but then there are the two other trees she's got up. I have to give it back to her if I'm ever thinking of throwing it away."

"I like it," said Will. He flicked the angel. Made her little arm wave. "The twins?"

Trace nodded. "They're doing my decorating," he said.

Of course, I thought. Why hadn't I seen it? The whole place was decorated in paper versions of the real thing. There were balls of white on the mantel arranged carefully around a little box filled with cotton. The baby Jesus inside was a twist tie bent into a green stick figure. On the built-in shelves there were a few cereal boxes pasted over with kid art, meant as books, I guessed. The slanted rectangle of paper on the couch was a remote for the television too old to receive its imagined signals.

"What do the girls think of this place?" I said.

"I don't know," said Trace. "At first they thought it was fun, but now that I don't come back home with them, they're unhappy about it."

"You're out of the house completely?"

"Just about," he said. "Most of our stuff was hers when it came down to it. The dogs she's keeping until I know what work looks like. She doesn't want them alone too much."

If Kara was thinking about letting the dogs go, it was serious. It was the dogs that had brought them together in the very beginning. They'd featured prominently on their first date, a story retold to the point of embarrassment. The glass of wine nosed over by the Boxer, the furious clean-up licking that always brought a high blush to Kara's pale face in the telling. *I was trying to pretend like I felt like cleaning it up and so was he,* she'd say, *and that's when we realized we weren't going out.* I didn't know what could have happened between them to bring on the separation, but I knew it as colossal. I knew it as elemental.

"I don't know what to say," I said. "It's just so sad. Could you ever have guessed your life would end up this way?"

Trace turned in place. Let his hands fall to his jeans with a slap. "You know, you don't have to say anything," he said. "I appreciate your sympathy, but I'm doing fine." He ducked down a hallway and switched on the lights in the kitchen. "I'm getting us some holiday drinks," he said. "Make yourselves comfortable."

Will was already sitting before the word *comfortable* had even registered with me. He'd taken the recliner and was glaring at me out of the mouth of his hood.

"What are you doing?" he asked in a scrappy whisper, a scolding sound I hadn't known he could do. He sounded like me.

"What do you mean?"

"He's trying to have a Christmas and you're messing it all up."

"By asking about the tree?"

"Forget it."

Trace was back. He had three sodas and a pack of Oreos. "I'd offer you something more appropriate," he

51

said. "But do I think the Oreos have red and green inside."

"Awesome," said Will. "I love those things."

And that was how it went. We ate the Oreos and Trace and Will joked about the filling, made out of hog tails and cow entrails. The hot dogs of cookies. Cookies even the dogs wouldn't eat. We were all carried happily along in our empty talk until the issue of custody arose. Will surprised me again by agreeing immediately to Trace's suggestion that he spend the weekends at his house from now on. "Cool," he said, as if that were all there was to it, as if I were merely a passenger in their conversation, somebody they were dropping off at the next stop.

The thing about Trace was that there was always a bit of the townie punk never grown up about him. He still drank all night in the yard with the boys, pitching empty cans into a fire ringed with bricks. He still raced derbies in old beaters and wore the same seven shirts he'd always worn. Noah had started out in a similar place, but he went hard straight. He looked at Trace and saw a former version of himself he now resented and considered a little dangerous. He felt he knew Trace to the core, knew every foul thing he'd done as a young man because he'd done it too. He'd been there at his side. And then of course Trace had done something

Noah would never do: He'd slept with his best friend's wife. No matter what Trace did now, Noah would never accept him as a man fit to be a father. He hid his contempt as best he could for Will's sake, but it was always there. You could feel it coming off of him in waves like heat when Trace was in the room. *Give me one reason.* I wondered how long I'd be able to dance Will around the inevitable fight now that Trace was back in town.

When we reached our drive, I said what I always said, "Hold on," and my arm went out involuntarily to hold Will back in his seat. Our house was up a steep incline, the kind you regret once it's cold. Black ice stood out if you knew how to look for it, the solid patches in the gravel, but seeing it didn't make it any less slick, like driving up runners. The house was a three-story farmhouse, over a hundred years old. Noah had moved it from its original lot at the base of the hill, where drainage had been a historically nagging problem. This move of thirty yards had been a year in the making. A project involving cranes and a crew of twenty. It was a wonder, the sound of the house lifting from its foundation. A moan I imagined as the foothill's reluctance to let loose an old, dark tooth. We'd made the paper that year, *The Athens News.* Will on my hip and Noah at my side, the house suspended above its empty cavity in the background. The picture was framed in the foyer, where we greeted the occasional guest. It was the first stop on the tour, the one room lit in the house as Will and I drove up the hill.

"Do you think he's up?" I asked.

Will didn't bother with a response. He was already imagining his room and his belongings in it. The tiny television near the foot of his bed and the blanket from his childhood he denied requiring for sleep. A warm space into which he could disappear, free from his attachment to me, my cloying thoughts, my concerns, my son, my son. He had the door open before I had the car in park.

"Goodnight," I said.

"Night."

Inside the kitchen, where I tossed my keys and purse, there was an empty wine bottle and cutting board, an orange slice of cheese going greasy and a stack of crackers. Noah wasn't in the living room, or the dining room, where he sometimes drank at the marbled wood table and did paperwork. His shoes were on the stairs, polished black with the socks stuffed inside. The sheets were turned down on the bed, but he wasn't there either. From our upstairs bathroom I could see the light on the back porch was on. Noah was sitting at the table on the patio, smoking a cigar. I could make out the thinning patch on the top of his head and the movement of his eyebrows as he puffed, blue smoke coming up like a signal. *Know that I am here*, it said, but it didn't give any further instruction. When I came out, he stood up from his chair. "It's cold," he said. "You didn't have to come out."

"It's OK," I said. "It's not too bad."

He pulled out one of the heavy metal chairs for me, dusted off a fine layer of snow. I sat and flipped the hood of my coat up. It was one of those high-tech zippered beasts, capable of beating out the coldest winds technically possible, something Will made me buy if I was going to persist in waiting for the bus with him. *At least stay warm while you're embarrassing me*, he'd said.

"How was Lancaster?" asked Noah. He was twisting his cigar in his oversized ashtray. I remembered it as one of last year's Christmas gifts. Like my gloves, like the boots Noah was wearing, like the tools swinging from the grill.

"It was something."

"Did Kara make everybody sing her original Kwanzaa and Hanukkah numbers?" he asked. "Did you have to wear the red sweaters for the pictures again? Was Trace wearing that hat?"

"He was wearing the hat."

"He bought that damn hat when we were teenagers," he said. "Bargained it off some bum on the street who played violin for money. I'm surprised it still holds together."

I watched the darkness settle around our circle of light on the porch. It was difficult to see the woods with any of the house lights on. Your eyes adjusted to one setting, refused another. There could have been a deer in those woods, a whole army of deer battling an army of silent hunters, and I wouldn't have known they were there. Noah pulled on his cigar and then seemed to consider it. It was an intentional sort of considering, the kind meant only to communicate itself, nothing more.

"You're awfully quiet," he said. "Did something happen?"

I wondered about my reluctance to tell Noah about Trace and Kara. Was I more concerned about what it might mean to our family, or what it might mean to him personally? What could it mean to Noah that Trace was again unattached, that he was again near, that Will and I had been in his house that evening, celebrating Christmas as a family, while Noah sat alone at home with the cats, not ten miles away, drinking a bottle of wine and slicing cheese in an empty kitchen? He always sliced the thinnest slips of cheese, as though to save us the larger part of everything he enjoyed.

"Trace and Kara are separating," I said.

Noah choked on a mouth of smoke and then laughed. "I'll bet that made for a happy holiday," he said. "Are they even talking to each other?"

"They're talking," I said. "You'd never guess anything was wrong when they're around the girls. But we went over to Trace's new place and it was not pretty."

"He moved out? It's that serious?"

"It seems serious. He's looking for work in town now and she's got her ring in a dish in the bathroom, right where anybody could see."

"That's like her," he said. "Talk about tact."

"She's an original. Nobody's denying that."

Noah leaned back in his chair and turned his head square to me. "Wait a minute," he said. "He's in town?"

"He's in the county," I said. "He's got a shithole rental. It looks like animals have been living in it. The furniture is all hauled up from their basement, probably the stuff he was using before they were married.

"You were there?"

"We went over there after we left Lancaster."

The night air stood around us in a pall of frost. I saw our lives suspended in it, long figures quiet in the cold. And I wanted it to stay there, to hold. "I'm so sorry," I said. My voice wavered, the flush of exhaustion pulling through it, and I held my mouth with a gloved hand as though to hold it all inside, all of my worrying.

"What are you sorry about?"

"I know you two don't get along. I knew you'd be upset."

Noah walked the length of the patio, the path of his boots a wide arch in the dust of ice on the cement. "Why would I be upset?" he asked. "Is there something else you're not telling me? He didn't try something on you, did he?"

"No, of course not," I said. I laughed and then hid inside the crisp bulk of my coat. "Nothing like that."

He brought his face near mine and found my eyes, made me look at him. "As long as you're telling me the truth, we have nothing to worry about. All I've ever asked from you is to be honest with me."

"Change can be upsetting," I said. "I felt like we had a nice thing going with Trace and his family in Chauncey. Now, who knows what will happen? Is Kara going to let us see those girls?"

"Why wouldn't she? You take things too seriously. You always have."

It was the usual complaint. Noah called it my nerves acting up. Will called it *mom freaking out*. I'd noticed, though, that it was generally lodged when one or the other of them wanted something badly enough. It was becoming more and more difficult to tell what that something was. They were onto me, shielding their weak spots, tucking up their loose threads. Noah stood behind me and shook my chair. "Do you want to help me finish this cigar, or should we go inside?"

"It's Christmas," I said. "I'll do whatever you want."

"That's your gift to me? Be still my heart."

He turned his cigar hard in the ashtray and took me by the hand inside. We locked the doors, front and back. We set the coffee machine and turned on the dishwasher. Together, we ate the cookies left out by the tree. We'd forgotten to eat them on Christmas Eve in the chaos of assembly, finally hanging the handlebars in place on the mountain bike with red ribbon and agreeing to let it be a future father-son project. We'd done the cookies every year of Will's life, though he'd discovered us at the age of seven, huddled over the plate. First, he said, "Why are you eating Santa's cookies?" and then he answered his own question. "You are Santa." A week later: "Do I still get presents if I don't believe?" We told him to pretend to believe. As though that was all that mattered anyhow and perhaps it was.

After closing up shop downstairs, we sat in bed reading instead of sleeping, both of us in our cheap, grocery-store reading glasses. Noah's habit of tracing each line of text with his finger as he read seemed to me a way of telling me he was upset without saying it. He traced half a page and then started again at the top. "Is there something you want to say?" he asked. "You're watching me read instead of reading."

"You're not reading either."

"What is it?" he asked. "You have to tell me now or we'll never get to sleep."

"Trace asked Will if he wanted to spend weekends at his place and Will said yes. Don't get angry."

Noah took off his glasses and placed them inside his book. "Will said yes?"

"Yes."

"What did you say?"

"They didn't ask me."

"Nobody asked me either."

"What do we do now?"

"I'll tell you exactly what we do," he said. He reached over his head and snapped out the light above his side of the bed. "We go to sleep. Because there's no way in hell that's ever happening." He put his book and glasses on the bedside table and turned on his side. In my own little halo of light, I imagined the dreams we'd both be having that night. The three of us are driving down the street and Trace is behind us in the distance. He's walking, but he's catching up.

Will was the sort of boy who needed prompting to move. I had to remind him to brush his teeth every day, to call his friends before he lost them, to have interests. The prospect of entertaining him for the week of vacation remaining before he had to return to school was one I'd always approached with an attitude of excitement and animation I supposed we all recognized as trumped up. *Together time,* I chortled. *Won't we have such fun?* I proposed trips to the skating rink, walks down to the river, art projects, visits to relatives in cities with Targets, only to be mocked. I needled to the extent I felt I was obligated to needle and then turned on the television with half-baked resignation. We had every channel, some of them German. If I felt daring, I asked Will what was going on with the shows. "What's this one about?" I'd ask. "Nothing," he'd say. I'd say, "That's what I thought." And we'd proceed happily into the New Year, pausing only to feed, to bathe. Noah always came home from his work at the real estate office and joined the laze proceedings seamlessly.

This year was different because every moment of inactivity had a barbed lining. More than once, my attempts at discussing Trace's new arrangements and the idea of weekends away had been rebuffed. *Mountain out of a molehill,* was the expression they were both using on me, as though they'd rehearsed dealing with me together, as if they had a game plan. Discussion had ended entirely when Noah demanded to know what I thought of him. "Do you think I'm going to let somebody like Trace disrupt my family? Is that what you think of me? He'll forget he even mentioned weekends. You watch," he said.

"He is Will's father," I said. "We have to respect that."

"Will knows who his father is," he said. He raised his nose, as though detecting something foul in the air. "No offense, Sister, but you are kind of creating a poisonous atmosphere here," he said.

"I'm poisonous?"

It was then that I'd become a cleaning dynamo, lifting dust before it settled on surfaces, cleaning the things I used to clean other things with. I reorganized the storage space in the basement and discovered three *Hustlers* rolled inside an oversized flowerpot. They were old, one of them featuring the concept of New Hippie Sex. Body paint and bean bags. Nudes strumming guitars in plush upholstered vans. At some point, they must have been Noah's, but I suspected Will had inherited them quietly. It was the kind of transmission that, if exposed, could damage us all inordinately. I replaced them and went upstairs to see what I could see. Will was spread on the living room couch, a bag of chocolate kisses on the floor and silver wrappers dotting his torso like tin acne. "Don't you want to do something?" I asked.

"Like what?"

"Have a friend over?"

"We're playing a game online at three."

"Oh," I said. There were three empty cans of soda on the end table and headless chocolate Santa in the basket with the coasters. "I thought I hid your stocking," I said.

"You did."

I'd been downstairs at dawn, too early for vacation week, with the sole intention of stealing away all of the holiday junk food. Will was putting on weight. Noah and I were both concerned, but according to one of the less fortunate *Rules Of Mom* agreements, I wasn't allowed to speak of it. Under my direction, we hadn't let on yet that we were monitoring his diet. The shift in the refrigerator and pantry had been subtle, the bright fluorescents easing into ruddy earth tones. Skittles turned to nuts. Trix to muesli, white to wheat. Will's only complaint thus far had been that he didn't like the fake milk or ice cream. *I don't know which one of you is lactose intolerant, but it's sucking for the rest of us*, he said. I'd hidden his Christmas candy where I thought he'd never find it: my medicine cabinet, which contained such horrors as tampons, hormone supplements, and shower caps.

"I guess you're onto me then," I said.

"You're kind of obvious," he said. I lifted his legs from the couch like a bridge and sat beneath them. "What?"

"I can't relax."

"No kidding," he said. "You're driving me and Dad crazy. It's like you're on crack or something."

"Crack? You think your mother is on crack?"

"You need to take a pill, Mom."

"Now you *want* me to do drugs?"

"Do something. We can't take it anymore."

"You've talked about this, the two of you?"

"We've noticed you're on edge. If it's because you're worried about Trace, you don't have to be. We talked it all out."

"Really," I said. "And what did you decide?"

"That there's nothing to decide. It is what it is."

It sounded like something Noah would say. Very resolute, very adult. I wondered if Will knew what he was saying, what it meant. On the television, young couples were climbing through bogs of filth, gathering yellow and red flags. I couldn't imagine what the point of that must be. I looked at my hands and discovered they were working at the pills in Will's sweats, snapping them at the base and smoothing them over.

"You're right," I said. "I should do something. Maybe I'll go for a drive. Think you could hold down the fort for an hour or two?"

He aimed the remote at me and pressed a button. I didn't have to see to know it was the giant, red OFF button. There was a fine layer of snow on the car I ignored and slid in neutral down the drive. I drove all over Athens at low, loitering speeds. Cruising. People went for drives when they needed to think, I knew, but I didn't know what people did when they needed not to think. When they were older and they drank only moderately on the approved occasions. When they had nothing, exactly, to be unhappy about except for mistakes they'd made before their only sons were born.

I drove up the hill to the old insane asylum, the Ridges. It was like a fortress of decay overlooking the tiny city. In the early 1800s it had featured micro-lakes at its base, islands the shapes of diamonds and hearts, clubs and spades, as though it were all a happy game happening in the land, while the crime of hysteria happened above. As a teenager I'd always been attracted to a particular ruin, a sandstone staircase that led to a rich elm. I considered it a pleasant metaphor. It was concealed now in snow, a white bulge in the surface that could have been anything.

I reclined my seat in the car and took in the plane of white sky. And I felt the kind of calm that can come when one compares life on the whole. In the spires behind my little red car, the saddest women of the last century had wailed. They'd been lobotomized for the crime of menopause and moodiness and buried in the graves marked only by white-washed stones of approximate shape and size. It became a habit that week, a ritual, this driving to the Ridges and reclining.

It began as another trade, another compromise, but very quickly it was something all my own. *I could have more of these things for myself*, I thought, *but where would I be?* No one ever asked me where I'd been when I got home. *Perhaps*, I thought, *I'm having an unexpected affair with myself.*

I took the relationship to the next level by booking a solo afternoon walking tour of the grounds. It was too cold for it and the ancient and Eddie Bauer-ed woman running the show—introduced only as The Official Guide—was clearly grumpy about the fact that I'd worn inappropriate shoes and a coat without a lining, and so I gave up midway through and told her I had hot cider in a Thermos in my car. Once safely ensconced with the heater blasting, The Official Guide and I became chatty. We were both locals and had somehow never met before or maybe had met and immediately determined one another wholly dismissible. She shared the juicy detail that many of the windowsills in the rooms that had once been cells were still carved with messages and dates, grooves carved by fingernails. There was a stain left by a dead woman's body in an attic. It was impossible to remove from the hardwoods.

"Do you think it's haunted?" I asked her. "Of course it's haunted. How could it not be haunted, all of those poor, damned people locked up in those little rooms?"

The Official Guide downed her cider and passed the cup that was also the lid back to me. "Mental illness is not a case of being haunted, or cursed, or damned like the people of this town still seem to think."

"Oh, of course not," I said. "I'm so sorry. That was very insensitive of me to say. The truth is that I feel a kinship with them. The women who were treated here. Lately, I mean."

"We really ought to know better by now," she said, "but, we don't. It's such a mess and I suspect it will continue to be a mess until we die. And then it will be done."

And that was that. She was out of the car and traipsing through the snow back to her cramped office that was now also a campus mail depot. And I sat there for hours. Hours and hours, just pondering what in the hell she might have meant by that. And then I decided she was wrong. It would not be a mess. Or, if it was a mess, it would be a beautiful mess. Or, if it was not a beautiful mess, it would at least be ours. Our mess.

On New Year's Eve, the culminating event of the vacation week that threatened never to end, I woke to find Noah at the kitchen table, eating a slice of leftover apple pie. "What are you doing?" I asked, tightening my robe at the waist.

"What does it look like I'm doing?" he asked. "I'm having a slice of pie."

"Will's on a diet," I said.

"But I'm not," he said. He licked the tines of his fork. "Or am I? Are you tricking us both into dieting? Has this been your plan all along?"

"I'm not tricking," I said. "I'm helping. And what is he going to think when he comes down here and sees you? Pie for Breakfast Day, is what he's going to think."

"He will not eat pie for breakfast."

"Watch him."

After I made coffee, we sat at the table together and picked through all the Christmas cards. There were very few from my family. They all lived in Athens and didn't see the point in mailing, when you could call or walk down the street. Noah's family in Kentucky had sent a ream of photo cards. The dog, the kid, the house, the three-runner, all photoshopped to heaven with holly berries, all glossy and piercingly arranged. They were such a pointy sort of people. I wondered at Noah's roundness in comparison. His easy nose and his cheeks like meaty palms. If we'd had a child together, (we'd given up and considered it fate after years of trying) it would have been his features dominating the face. His heart mouth over my crooked teeth. His bright eyes lighting out my dark face. I knew this in the way you know what kind of sound you'll make before you speak.

But somehow Will and Noah always had a certain dusky resemblance, which made life less difficult. Everyone always assumed they were father and son, uncomplicated. And when the old ladies in the Kroger's would tell Will he looked just like his father, the pair of them would always smile their big-toothed smile. A joke between them meant to heighten their resemblance. A sharky sort of face.

"Do you remember that smile you and Will used to do?" I asked. "When people said he took after you?"

"What made you think of that?"

"Looking at these pictures," I said. "You used to do it in the family shots and I'd always have to retake them." I held up a shot of Noah's nephew. He was in full motocross regalia, a tiny motorcycle leaning into his thighs. You might guess he was happy, the smile lost beneath the orb-like helmet. A spindly woman in a white tank top angled in a lawn chair behind him, her bare feet in the grass. His mother, I realized, Noah's sister. "Why would you pick this one for a Christmas card?" I asked.

"Look at that kid. What kind of person puts his kid on a bike at that age? They're hicks. Straight-up Kentucky hicks."

"We're Ohio hicks," I said.

"Big, big difference," he said.

I shooed him with the photo, threw it back into the pile. Noah picked it up and made like he was aiming to pitch it in the trash. "Don't even think about it," I said. He paused, like I'd caught him in a dilemma and then Will came down the stairs in the rush that always scared me, sounding like a sack of bricks and rocks rolling down. He slid into the kitchen in the new sweat suit that made him look like a giant, dark cloud. It was his alter ego, the only way I could get out of having to wash the usual hoodie every day.

"What are you two fighting about?" he asked. "I could hear you all the way upstairs." He walked to the refrigerator and opened it.

"Your father thinks his family is trash," I said.

"They are pretty trashy, Mom. Let's face it."

"Anyway, we weren't fighting," I said. I felt a drip of coffee run down my chin and was too late to stop it. "Why would we be fighting?"

"Fine, fine. You weren't fighting," he said. He rummaged through a few Tupperware containers. "Where's the rest of that pie?"

I sighed. "When you're finished with that pie, I want you to eat something nutritious," I said. "Both of you." I walked to the refrigerator and pulled out four good eggs, the soymilk, the low-fat turkey sausage. They were behind me, making faces. I could feel it. Their hands were at their throats, their tongues curved out. In a few minutes, Will and I would be aping Noah behind his back, mimicking his breakfast rituals, the napkin spread carefully over his lap, the three brisk shakes of salt on his eggs. And then maybe Noah and I would be on Will about showering. We'd tell him he smelled. That the natural grease he claimed made his hair look good was beginning to take over his entire head. *You look like a grit,* we'd say. *We didn't raise a grit.* The teams would rotate naturally and evenly, nobody landing anywhere solidly. You never knew who'd stand with whom, but you could bet there'd be an odd one out.

"What are we doing for New Year's?" asked Will.

"I don't know. The usual, I guess," I said. The usual consisted of inviting a few of Will's friends over to bang pots and pans in the drive at midnight, but I'd assumed he'd outgrown that this year and foregone the calling and planning. "Do you need me to call some moms?"

"I was kind of thinking we could go and see Trace's pad today," said Will.

Noah and I looked at each other, eyebrows high. I had the thought that I should breathe, breathe somehow, but I lost that thought. It broke off like a leaf and scuttled across the kitchen.

"Pad?" said Noah. "His *pad?*"

"Sure," said Will. "His bachelor pad."

"Forget it, Will," I said.

"You've been on pins and needles all week," he said. "This can't go on. We've got to go over there and put on a good face. For all of our sake's."

"Will's right," said Noah. "Solidarity."

I doubted a visit to Trace's would solidify a thing. How could it? But I found myself outnumbered and overpowered. Both of them were hyped up about visiting Trace. Pumped. They wanted to bring him a lava lamp. Will thought Trace should have a dartboard. I searched behind Noah's excitement and found no motives I could call exactly ulterior. "If Will wants to go, we'll go," he said. Then, in response to my incredulity, "Look, I'm curious to see what it looks like too, OK? Both of you have seen this place, but I haven't." He held up his hands as if to show me the nothing he had up his sleeves. If he was acting, he was doing a very good job of it. He said he had some beer he thought would be good for housewarming, a Belgian formula, brewed by Trappist monks. He had an old tapestry in the basement he thought was bachelor material. I knew Trace couldn't cook and wasn't likely to take very good care of himself without Kara around. "I guess I could bring Trace a plate of leftover turkey," I said.

"Then it's decided," said Noah. "We're visiting Trace."

It took far too long for us to realize that we didn't have a number for Trace at his new place and he was not and had never been the cell phone type. We were suited up and standing in the foyer before we realized we should give him fair warning if we were coming. We knew Kara would have his number, but we didn't know how to broach the topic and then get off the phone without getting sucked into an hour-long chat. Will and Noah had decided that I should call her and pretend to be interested in one of her art projects, maybe the bright pink plastic and wire mobiles she was selling in the consignment shops around town, and set up a time to talk more about them. "How cruel," I said. "You want me to feign an interest in her art?" I thought of Kara's tendency to over-share, her insistence that we treat each other as sisters might. "I'm not calling her. The last thing I want to do today is talk to Kara about her separation from Trace."

"Don't talk about the separation," said Will. "Don't bring it up."

"If I call out of the blue and I don't say something about it, she'll think I'm being weird or insensitive. She'll be hurt," I said.

"What else are we going to do?" asked Will. "Stand here in our coats and listen to one end of the worst conversation possible?"

"I'm not calling her," I said. "And I know you don't want to call her either. So, here we are." I unzipped and threw my purse on the table.

"Let's just go," said Noah. "If he's there, you can ring the bell and ask him if he's up for a visit. You can tell him we were at the Sears over there and decided to stop by."

"Why me?" I asked.

"Do you want me to show up at his door unannounced?" he asked. I thought of that possibility, of what Trace might think, if only for a moment. "No, I'll do it," I said. Noah opened the door and ushered us all through it. The drive from Athens to Chauncey was strangely energized. There were seven miles of houses between ours and Trace's and almost every one of them was still tinged with silver and gold balls and pulses of colored lights. We slowed to admire the most ambitious of holiday displays, something we hadn't done since Will was very little. He'd called the lights, *gights*, then and pointed with a tiny red finger. *Gights, gights*. There was one house in particular we'd always made a point of hitting. The owners must have been boat people, a thing we found odd given the general state of the Hocking River—rarely more than a sludged trickle. We pulled up to find that they'd carried on the tradition. There were two boats set up in the yard, their weathered bodies strung with lights. Inside one of the boats, The Longernecker, a glowing Santa waved. Inside the other, The Chastity, a full plastic nativity set sat awkwardly, each of the figures wound up with gold tinsel. "They're there," said Will. "I can't believe they still do this."

"What is wrong with these people?" I asked. "What are they thinking?"

"They're crazy," said Will.

"I think it's beautiful," said Noah. Beautiful. I couldn't remember the last time he'd used that word on anything but a notable play in a football game. His face was bright and calm, a gauzy distance in his eyes. Maybe he'd finally lost it and found the true meaning of Christmas in this lopsided gleaming show, or maybe he meant to undercut our cynicism, expose it as cruel. And maybe we *were* cruel, imagining ourselves as superior to these people for their blatant enthusiasm. Our decorations had always been pared back and conservative, white and silver, as though to celebrate without embracing. Maybe we were the frauds. At least this family had picked a side.

"Maybe there's a lesson to be learned here," I said.

"Actually, I think it's fucking hysterical," said Noah. "Who puts boats in their yard for Christmas?"

"We are terrible people," I said. I leaned my head into the dash. Will couldn't get over Noah's free use of the word *fuck*. "Fucking hysterical," he said. "I can't believe you said that. It is fucking hysterical. That's exactly what it is." We passed the Sears and considered, briefly, a stop to back up our story, a few bags to sit in

75

the front of the car as props, and then realized that too as fucking hysterical. Will said *fuck*, until we told him to stop, and then he said *fuck* again. *Fuck, fuck, fuckidy fuck. Merry fucking Christmas.* A warped kind of caroling. When we pulled into Trace's long drive, I found myself hoping he was home, wishing it. I was giddy with the notion of us all being happy together. I imagined myself in the role of the spokesperson pegged to deliver the giant check. One made out in the amount of *Your Happy Family*, to recipient Trace Williams. "Can you believe you've won?" I'd ask. "I can't believe it," he'd say. "Nothing like this ever happens to me." I squeezed Noah's hand on the wheel and opened the car door.

"We'll stay here until you come back and give us the OK," he said.

"Look for a hand signal," I said. "Something around the head."

"Got it," said Noah. "Ten-four."

Trace's car was in the drive, but there weren't any lights on inside the house. I had to walk around the side yard to get to the light of the porch, a yellow ball in the grey light of the day. I knocked on the door and listened for movement inside. It was cold. Ohio cold. Wet and thick. It got under your coat, slipped up your pant leg. I was about to knock again when I saw a light come on in the living room. Trace pried apart the blinds and peered through. I waved, marching in place to keep my legs warm. He put one finger up, saying, one minute, and I nodded.

There was a collapsing inside, items shuffled about hurriedly, and it struck me that Trace might not be alone. Maybe there was someone else? Maybe that's what was at stake in his marriage? Why hadn't it occurred to me? I imagined his embarrassment, the woman inside, rushing her face on in the mirror. He'd be hiding the whiskey they'd been drinking, emptying cigarette butts into the trash. And then Will would be there and he'd have to explain. He'd have to introduce this person, this newest member to our messed-up clan. He'd have to face Noah's judgment. His terrible, acrid judgment. *Merry fucking Christmas and happy fucking New Year.*

He opened the door with half his shirt tucked in and the buttons done wrong. His hair was wild and he hadn't shaved. "Trace, are you alone?"

"Yes," he said. "I'm alone."

"Really?"

He opened the door wider to let me look around inside, see for myself.

"Thank God," I said. My smile beamed so big I could feel it pull away from my face and almost drift into the snow. "It seemed like such a good idea to come here and then I knocked and I realized there might be somebody else here. Somebody you were seeing," I said.

"No, of course I'm not seeing anyone."

"Good. I mean, that's great," I said. I was smiling again, like some wild ray had possessed my face. It was my will for us to be happy, to be set right. For the perpetual negotiations to end.

"You came out here to visit me?" he asked. "Today? Now?"

I nodded and smiled, hopping in place to stay warm, and then he was moving me inside the house with a swiftness that I assumed was concern for the cold until he had me pinned against the wall, a hot knee between my thighs. He held my chin between his thumb and forefinger. "Is this real?" he asked. "Is this happening now?"

My heart pounded in my ears. I hadn't been this close to Trace in well over a decade, but my mouth knew what to do when it met his, how to meet the hard challenge of his need. This wasn't a normal kind of kissing; it was two bodies colliding in space and we were inside and outside of each other and then stood there destroyed and panting.

"I think maybe you got the wrong idea," I said, finally.

"That didn't feel wrong to me," he said.

"The boys thought it would be a good idea to come and see you," I said, swallowed.

"Oh, God."

He closed his eyes and released me. It was then that I smelled the whiskey. I smelled the cigarettes. And I understood how the night had passed for him. I'd had one such night myself. He'd seen the miserable state I was in and had pitied me, had done what I'd asked, which was to love me for the space of a night. And now here I was, repeating the same scene all these years later, appearing on his porch out of nowhere, only I had no love to give him. Instead, I came bearing the gift of the most awkward hours he'd ever passed in his life. When he opened his eyes, I was looking straight into them, understanding.

"I'm an idiot," I said. "I want to kill myself for coming here like this."

"Wait a minute," he said. "Let's not get excited." He pointed a finger over my shoulder. His lips were thick with wet. "Are Noah and Will *here* here? In the car right now?"

"Yes," I said. "They're both out there in the car."

He pressed on his eyelids and breathed into his sleeve. "Let me fix things up and then they can come inside. Five minutes. Would that be OK?"

"That would be fine."

"Maybe ten minutes. And you should tend to your face."

The door shut firmly and I saw my own reflection in the lock-plate well enough to know that my best bet was a fist full of snow around the mouth and a quick wipe with a sleeve. No time for careful ministrations. I had a medicated chapstick in my pocket and I thanked the Lord for the potency of its cherryness as I slathered it on. When I back got inside the car, Noah was sitting on his hands to keep them warm. Will was doing the same. His legs were going in his perpetual jog, the one that never took him anywhere. And I saw with a clarity I'd never before had why that was, why he was dancing all the time. If we were to go inside, Noah and Will would see Trace at his weakest. One would feel his righteousness rigor in his spine and the other would have a choice to make, the right father to follow this time. I saw Will's heart, saw it as clearly as his strained face, as the lip he always chewed with his upper teeth, his eyes that rarely met an adult's. He was caught because he was a good son and because he had hope. How I'd underestimated him. How I'd failed to see his struggle as his own.

"Is everything OK?" asked Noah.

"We should go," I said.

"Maybe I should talk to him," he said. "Make sure."

"Drive the car," I said. I pointed at the steering wheel. "Right now."

He hesitated and then eased up in a tight perch. "Alright," he said. "But we're talking about this."

"Just drive," I said.

I let the silence sit on us for a mile or two before I spoke, waiting for real seriousness to set in. Every muscle in Noah's back was pulled tight. He drove like we were in a massive semi.

"Trace isn't doing very well," I said.

"Is he sick?" asked Will.

"He just spent the first whole week away from his wife and his family. Can you imagine what that must have been like for him?"

I waited for the reply I knew I wouldn't get. They'd assume I'd think they were obediently imagining how that would be in their silence. The truth would be a shade darker. They'd both be seeing the week from another family's perspective—ours. Who could blame them?

"What's going on?" asked Noah.

"I told you," I said. "He isn't feeling well. He said to say hello to both of you and we'll do a visit some other time."

"He said to say hello to me?" said Noah. "See, I don't buy that. He'd never tell you to say hello to me."

"Fine, I lied," I said. "He said to say hello to Will. He said *you* could go fuck yourself."

Noah leaned up in his seat, brought his hand to his chest, let it fall. "He's a mess, isn't he? He's been drinking. I ought to bash his face in and give him a reason to drink," he said. "He's got kids to think about."

"Stop," I said. "Do not say another word."

We drove the remaining few miles in silence and when we pulled into the drive, Noah and Will were out of the car before I'd collected my things. There I was again, outside, while the two of them were inside. I sat there, I don't know how long, trying to figure out how to get back in there. My purse was in my lap and my hand was on the plastic bag of leftover turkey I'd prepared for Trace at my feet. Eventually, Will appeared at the door without his coat. He squinted his eyes and crossed his arms into his chest. "Aren't you coming in?" he asked. When I didn't reply, he hurried across the yard and got in the car. Out of habit, perhaps, he took a seat in the back. There we were, two passengers without a driver. Where could we go from here?

The winds were strong and they swayed us in the car. Our Christmas lights were on, the careful shapes Noah had made in the trees, and the star with strands of lights streaming into the snow.

"Chauffeur," I said. I gestured to the empty seat beside me. "To the Ritz."

"And I'll be having my champagne in the bath," said Will.

"Would you consider taking a meal on the veranda?"

"It's cold outside," said Will, and I feared our time there had ended. He'd make a joke now, make a bargain. He'd escape my plea, my ploy. He'd escape me.

"No," he said. "Have them serve it in the study."

III.

In the dreams I was always up to something so transgressive and wicked that in my waking life I carried a boulder of shame between my shoulders for weeks. It would start out ordinarily enough, a scene of myself dusting in the bedroom, let's say. A depressingly domestic vignette that included, perhaps, the use of that special extendo tool and the cobwebbed corners of the eaves, and then I would be fucking Trace while Noah watched, fucking Trace while Noah watched, fucking Trace while Noah watched. To be clear, this was a scenario that would never—ever—play out in real life. Middle-age may have dampened both men, but they still regularly scuffled over one perceived slight or another. Noah was famous for publicly threatening Trace's life. It was *a whole thing* in town. And so the idea that I'd fuck one while the other watched was insane. Ludicrous. I would have gladly died before granting such a dream free access to my mind. And yet, whenever it arrived upon me, the dream was so cell-agitating as to render me spiritually rejuvenated upon waking.

Have you ever orgasmed in your sleep? I never knew this was possible until I started having this dream. To be honest, I'd given up on orgasms. Like push-up bras, they no longer seemed worth the bother. I should be clear: Noah was in the process of dying of cancer. We were about two years into the mess. In the beginning, we all thought he would beat it. We were, perhaps, even a little cavalier about the prospect of his full recovery. If anyone could beat lung cancer it would be Noah, the man who once drove for twenty hours straight to see his son deliver one line in a college play. The man who competed in competitions involving axes well into his forties. The man whose nickname was Iron Face for his ability to refrain from blinking during intense lathing sessions. But once he moved permanently to the hospital—he would never again come home with me to our old, creaking beast of a house on a hill—we had to admit that we were wrong. He would die soon and he was very determined that I should not fuck Trace.

He made his position on this quite clear soon after we'd determined that hospice was the right next step. It was during one of our final back-patio sessions. We were both wrapped in thick blankets and rocking in chairs he'd made with his own hands and watching the sorbet-colored sunset and I was trying not to cry for the sheer beauty and tragedy of it. I'd married Noah so young that I could not imagine a life without him, simply could not fathom it, but moments like these were making me feel as though I'd had *enough* to call our life a good one. *Enough* was the word I repeated in my head. It had to be *enough* because he could no longer fight and I could no longer ask him to.

"All that I ask is that it isn't Trace," he said.

"What are you talking about?" I asked, startled. I was crying without knowing I was crying again, which was something that happened frequently enough then that I no longer attempted to explain or account for the wetness. I wiped my face in my hands and asked him again. "Noah," I said. "What in the hell?"

"I know you won't want to be alone. You're not built for it. You never were."

I scoffed, offended.

"It's not a judgment. It's the truth. You want to argue it? Go ahead. Use up what little time we have left with pretending."

He was right. It was the reason why I'd been fostering an absurd number of cats and dogs and even rabbits in our home. I was prepping for the emptiness. The crisp crisis of aloneness. I would not, could not be alone. But I had never considered inviting another man to take his place, much less Trace. The primary regret in my life was that I'd been with Trace, but it was a vexed regret because being with him had given us our only child. If I had not been with Trace, we would not have Will, of course. And without Will, our lives would have been fundamentally boring and meaningless. We would have grown old hating each other for our failures. Trace was a necessary evil. He was also wild and unkempt. For more than twenty years I'd been wondering what his inability to adult properly meant about me.

"Let me get this straight," I said. "You're fine with the idea of me starting up with someone new when you're gone, just not—" Here, I went into a deep sob. It went on long enough that he was irritated and finished my sentence for me.

"If heaven is a thing and I'm looking down and I see you with him, just know that I will be angry enough to curse the both of you forever. I will haunt you if I can." Later, he said, "I wish the best for you, I really do. But that is the one thing I cannot abide."

I told him I'd never be with Trace, that it was ridiculous to even think of it, that I was angry that he'd spoken this fear aloud, but he said again the bit about heaven. "I'll be watching," he said. "Know that."

And I suppose that's how it started. The dream. I had it for the first time that night and I had it almost every night thereafter. During the denouement of Noah's illness, it was like a horny alarm clock going off in the night. And the way that it made me feel in that sorrowful splay of time was alive. Alive and guilty as hell. Like a priest who has impregnated a nun.

In one novel iteration of the dream, I was in the bed of my old pick-up truck with Trace. I reached for him and he resisted at first but then he gave way and a wild, furious ache unfurled in my sleeping. The weird thing in this version of the dream was that Noah wasn't there at first, but then he was driving the truck and watching us, his eyes steeled in the rearview. *I'm going to have to issue a citation*, he always said. Sometimes he added, *little lady*. Like a cowpoke in a Western. Why oh why was my unconscious mind doing this to me?

By the time I was in my forties, the fact of my infidelity had been re-litigated so many times as to render me frankly numb to any aspersions anyone might think to cast. Whore, slut, fool—I'd heard them all and I'd heard them from issued from the mouths of women from every corner of the county—PTA bitches to my own mother. I had said all of the Hail Mary's one woman can say and I'd even done cognitive behavioral therapy to banish certain destructive *patterns of thought*. But one under-investigated territory was the fact that it was the best sex of my life. There was no comparing what happened that night to what happened before or after that night.

Further additions to the dream-generating shame heap included the fact that Trace had been in love with me since high school. This little nugget of awful had squeaked out during a particularly humid birthday pool party for the twins. I accused him of having a terrible memory for details because he'd mistaken one twin's favorite color for the other's and he said: *I remember what you were wearing the first time I saw you. Your jeans were pegged at the ankle and you had a side ponytail. You wore a knit cap that was made to look like a strawberry.* He crushed his can of beer against his thigh, pitched the empty over his shoulder, and opened another. *I remember everything,* he said.

Noah leaned into my ear and said: *If he ever mentions that hat again, I will beat him to death with his own shoe.*

I knew Trace had been waiting his whole adult life for a different life to happen to him and that different life was me, but I didn't love him like that. I'd never loved him like that. I knew that if I chose to be with him it would only be because I'd consented to abuse him for a time. Maybe I was weak enough to go there and maybe he was broken enough to let me, but we both knew it would be a disaster if we were together and so we relied upon Noah to violently enforce the boundary between us. Now that it was clear Noah was leaving us, he'd done us both the great favor of threatening to haunt the living shit out of me. It was his way of making his passing easier. It was devastatingly beautiful and spectacularly stupid at the same time.

Whenever Noah called me from the hospital it showed up in my phone as CALLER OBSCURED. I didn't know why this was and I asked the hospital staff and they didn't know either. Early on, Noah and I joked that it sounded like the name of a stupid band. Toward the end, though, it felt like he was calling from a place I could never get. Usually, he wanted to know where I was and what I was doing (he was often bored though reluctant to bother me), but this time he said he wanted all of his books packed up and donated to our tiny local library. He wanted me to make nameplates and paste them inside each book so that others would know that the titles were drawn from his—and he used these exact words—*personal library*. I decided to ignore the fact that we didn't have a library, let alone a personal one. We had numerous careening piles of books surrounding our bed.

"What if I want our books?" I asked. "Can I donate them to myself?"

He sighed. He was tired. It exhausted him to have to do these things, to acknowledge the loose threads still dangling. "Your books are your books. You know which ones they are."

"Fine," I said. I was already deciding whether or not I would respect this wish. I was, generally speaking, very accommodating of his directives. I'd even agreed to forgo a reception after the funeral. He wanted it easy and simple—even though it wasn't for him and dozens of loved ones would be disappointed and hungry. But maybe I wanted to keep some of *his* damn books and read them too.

"How are the animals doing?" he asked. He was changing the subject, plowing through my resistance.

"Fine," I said. I wanted to tell him about the animals, the precarious art of fostering beasts you're not allowed to love fully, but I couldn't because I needed to show him that I was mad.

"Any luck with placements this week?"

"No."

"OK," he said. "It sounds like you're busy. I'll see you later today?"

"Yes."

I pressed the hang-up button. The thing I did next was weird, very weird. I couldn't explain it to myself, but that's the thing about grief. It's like a spell. You can't control it even if you're the one casting it. I let all of the small animals out of their cages and let them do whatever they wanted for a while. Mostly, they chewed on forbidden items and pissed and shat. I didn't intervene. I merely watched, observed. And then I rigged up some porn on my laptop. Girl-on-girl, though I'm not a lesbian. I simply found the straight kind of porn unnerving—the shaved depravity of it all.

You'll have to invent the specific details of the very worst dream on your own because I'm not sharing them. That's not something I do: graphic sexual detail. You get the basic scenario (high school prom) and the players involved (me, my husband, the father of my son). That's it. *Deal with it*—something Noah would say. He was a no-nonsense kind of person. He didn't play around. He wasn't always that way. When we met, he was loose and free. His mother said she'd ground him if he didn't start tying his laces and so he threw away all of his laces and went flopping around in gap-tongued shoes. But then he had a son and the son began life in the NICU, born early and unable to breathe or eat on his own, and Noah became the laced-up person he still was at the end. He viewed aberrations in "normal" behavior as threats to his existence. This was one reason why cancer was so difficult for him to face. It was a mistake. Cells misfiring, multiplying. And he couldn't stop it or fix it and that would have been difficult for anyone, but it was especially difficult for a person like Noah.

When your spouse moves into hospice, you essentially separate. No one tells you this. The average stay is about six months and only a few days of this stay involve what they call *active dying*. Noah was not there yet and it was impossible for me to live in hospice with him, so I visited him daily or every other day if life happened to be hectic for one reason or another. When I was there, I read to him or we streamed a show together, or we made arrangements (his wishes were specific and stringent), or I cried while he sat in silence or slept. At home, I tended to animals and ate microwaved bags of food. We had doting friends and family members. In the beginning, they organized a parade of casseroles. But then the empty and washed casserole dishes stacked on the front porch for pickup became mingled with the new and full casserole dishes and the grim, marching reality of hospice care sunk in and then they simply texted me to ask how he was. *Status report please.*

I'm not going to lie: I was lonely. I found myself forcing people in the service industry to conversate with me. The mailman began dropping the mail at the end of our driveway because he was fatigued by my small talk. And so I had to go out to find fresh prey, which is how I wound up talking to Kara, without realizing I was talking to Kara, at the chic new vintage shop on the main drag. In my defense, she had adopted a new look. She was punk for twenty years and then suddenly she was glam. Blonde wig and matte-red lips. Plus, she'd lived all the way out in Chauncey forever and had always claimed she'd rather be caught dead than hang out in A-town because the Ohio U kids were so cloying.

"Are the 90s really back?" I asked her, not realizing it was her yet. "I mean, can we stop this from happening somehow? I don't want to revisit that decade. Bad things happened in that decade. I did bad things. The worst things. I wore overalls with only a tank bra underneath."

"Sister," she said. "You do realize you're talking to someone who actually knew you in the 90s, right? You definitely weren't an overalls and bra girl. You were a pink thermal with a jean skirt girl."

"Oh, hi, Kara," I said. "I didn't realize you were here."

She ignored the intentional ambiguity in my response—did I mean *here* in this chic new shop or *here* in this conversation or still hanging around *here* on this planet?—and rested her head between her hands, elbows on the glass display case that separated her from the artfully arranged do-dads and Doc Martens dotting the place.

"I heard about Noah," she said. "I'm so sorry. For what it's worth, I always thought he was a decent person."

"He's still alive," I said.

"What?"

"You said you thought he *was* a decent person. He's not dead yet, so you can still use the present tense on him."

Her eyes filled with tears and I immediately regretted my honesty. It wasn't her fault we didn't talk to each other or see each other anymore. We used to be something like family, but she and Trace had endured a bitter, blow-up kind of divorce and then all of the kids grew up and moved away and we had nothing in common and never really enjoyed each other's company in the first place. And then of course there was the thing in the past, the oft-re-litigated infidelity that bound me to Trace. Once, in a red-wine-sloshed moment, Kara confessed that she saw me as the other woman even though that wasn't entirely accurate. I was *a* woman. I was in the picture. But I was only with Trace once and that was well before her time. Of course, there was that kiss. The Kiss. But Kara and Trace were separated by then and I was sure no one knew about it because if anyone had known about it, Noah would have found out about it and the whole town would have gone up in flames.

"Please don't cry about it," I said. "It was an easy mistake. He's been in the hospital for a long while now. How could you know? It's not like we talk."

"The girls give me reports from time to time. Is it worse that they think he's dead too?" Now she was fully crying, banging around behind the counter in search of tissues. "It *is* worse. We, all three of us, have a callous streak, I know. Trace calls it the evil harpy strain."

"Well," I said. "I don't know if evil harpy is fair, but, yes, I do think it's worse. I mean, wouldn't you have gone to the funeral? Sent a card? Surely we're not that out of touch."

Kara gave up on her search and wiped her nose on her sleeve. I might have been disgusted before my era of involuntary crying, but now I appreciated her pragmatism. "I think we are," she said. "That out of touch, I mean. The girls see Will, which is good. He makes the effort. You raised him right, that one. But I haven't seen any of you in years. The last time we talked, we made plans to have coffee, but then I called you and your number was disconnected."

My mind groped through the past for evidence of a long-ago thwarted coffee date and returned only information regarding the change in phone numbers. "Oh my god, that was five years ago when we changed the phones. It was because of some deal Noah got. I thought we contacted everyone."

"Not everyone," she said. She softened. "It's fine. I don't drink coffee anyway."

"You don't? I could have sworn we had coffee together."

"We did. But, I don't drink it. Terrible reflux."

"You mean you endured terrible reflux because I was too daft or self-involved to listen when you told me you didn't drink coffee? And then I made you accept a

95

coffee date you didn't want and then changed my phone number on you?"

She smiled.

"I must be an asshole," I said.

She smiled again. "Yes, but I'm an asshole too, so we're even."

"Even," I said. And I wondered if that would ever be true. We had children with the same man, a man neither of us were with, and we were different in ways that drew forth the other's flaws. Kara was actually the type to wear a tank bra with massive overalls in the 90s. I was the type to observe her type and church-mouth her to the other girls. "I'm sorry about all of it," I said. I saw my full meaning register in her face. This was an apology that went back to the beginning.

She ran her thumbs beneath her eyes and they came away orange with foundation or bronzer or whatever. "Can I ask you something, Sister?"

Whatever her question was, I didn't want to hear it, but I nodded.

"Have you ever done anything that you *haven't* regretted? Maybe it's time to stop apologizing. Try to enjoy yourself. I mean it. You should try having a life for once—while you still have a chance."

I thought about asking her how much she enjoyed working for minimum wage in a store doomed to fail once the next wave of nostalgia hit, how she enjoyed her various addictions to pain pills and alcohol, how she enjoyed life as an afterthought in her own family, the kind of mother who heard from her kids only on her birthday and holidays. But I didn't. "I'll give you my number just so you have it," I said. "You don't have to call me, but you should definitely have it." I picked up a pen from the counter and wrote my name and number on the back of a stray receipt. "Is yours still the same?" I asked.

She nodded as she folded the receipt into her pocket. "Give Noah my best, will you? I really do hope he pulls through."

"He won't, but you're nice to say that," I said. "It makes me remember what it was like to carry around false hope."

And then the little bell over the door rang and I drove my car to Trace's place. I didn't let myself acknowledge to myself that I was there to talk to him about the dream, but that's what I was there to do. He wasn't home and it was weird to sit in my car in his driveway while the dogs lost their minds barking at me, so I drove home and went to bed at 4 p.m. in the afternoon. With the laptop.

The dream very often came nestled between other dreams—most of which involved excruciatingly domestic and mundane anxieties. Maybe I was running out of the sensitive kind of toothpaste again and headed to the store but the store was French-language-only or I was trying to vacuum but the machine was a tiny doll vacuum and it would take me centuries to do the first floor and then—I don't know how or why—I'd be fucking Trace while Noah watched, fucking Trace while Noah watched, fucking Trace while Noah watched. And then I'd bloop back out to the most boring and inane dreams possible. Maybe I'd be catching up with email, power-washing the drive, chasing pets around the yard but the pets are candy bars. Night after night after bloody lonely night.

In the leadup to the journey to hospice there had been conversations with Noah in which he had revealed his transgressions—most of them exceedingly minor. He conceded to driving far too aggressively, for example, and to cursing far too often. "I like using threatening words and phrases," he said. "It's the same with a vehicle." He also said he regretted that he wasn't, on the whole, more kind. "It wasn't that I felt it beyond me," he said. "Kindness was beneath me." The talks were his way of clearing his conscience and forging a more tidy path to his end.

He wasn't religious and so a priest would do him no good and he knew it was possible he'd eventually lose coherence—especially once the morphine came into the picture. He did not wish to be beset upon by a sense of regret he would be too far gone to parse. In other words, he feared babbling like a worried fool and botching his final confessions. The more serious admissions of guilt came in highly strained moments, moments announced as *moments*, as in, "we're going to have a moment here, Sister," and I learned to brace the innermost muscles of my heart against quaking.

He admitted to playing around with the stock market in a way that could have impacted us dramatically. I said I was sure it was nothing, but he said it could have lost us the house, Will's shot at his private college, the considerable savings that were now supposed to ferry me to my next phase of living—whatever in the hell that was supposed to be without him. He'd done it simply because he could, he said, because he was a small-town prick without a college education who wanted to show the finance guys in Columbus that his money was as good as theirs. And once he'd corrected his mistake, made back all of the money he'd lost and more, he'd vowed never to do it again. "I am proud to say I kept that vow," he said.

It was weird knowing that I'd once been on the brink of losing it all without knowing it. I thought of my ignorant face, laughing it up at the dinner table that could have been sold off at auction the next day. I couldn't quite bring myself to be mad, though. "I don't think I'd have cared, really," I said. "I've never cared about stuff."

"I know," he said. "But I would have cared. It would have killed me to go back."

By *back* he meant the early days of our marriage when he'd worked at a guitar factory for minimum wage, he meant his childhood punctuated by spells of hunger and cold, he meant the friends we still saw around but considered a bit too ragged for regular company. He'd made a lot of money in real estate—mainly by leveraging his understanding of the ebbs and flows that characterize an Appalachian college town—and was leaving me with enough savings to take as many Alaskan Cruises as I wanted. So much of his pride was wrapped up in that last fact that I could hardly stand it. Perhaps it was true that I required this kind of soft-gloving, but I didn't like to have to know it. "I would have loved you even if you'd stayed as broke as the day I met you," I said. "But I have enjoyed the luxuries you've provided." He reminded me that my face cream cost as much as a fancy meal at Purple Chopstix and I threw him a bone: "Once you develop a taste for the finer things in life, it's difficult to appease your desires with Noxzema."

It wasn't until he'd been in hospice for weeks, though, that he finally addressed what he'd once characterized as the greatest transgression of his life and it happened by text message at 3 a.m. in the morning: *I accused you of cheating because I had a mind to cheat myself. I've never admitted that.* I was awake and poking around on social media when the phone buzzed in my hand. I could have ignored the message and given myself the morning to recover, but I didn't. I responded immediately: *You're a lousy SOB and I forgive you.* He sent what was, I think, his first emoji, a laughing-crying face. And then he called. His voice was barely a whisper, a rasp. "We had a good time, though, didn't we?"

"Yes," I said. I was crying and it was the most I could get out of myself.

"Do you ever wish you'd run away and done something different with your life? You felt trapped sometimes, I think."

It was true, but I didn't know that he knew. I thought back to the devastation I'd done to my home and myself in the wake of his announcement that he was leaving me with a small stack of cash and a house full of useless-to-me belongings. I'd wanted to end it, delete that version of myself. Deep down, I wanted it all gone, destroyed so that I couldn't go back to it and would be forced to edge outside of the painful loop in which six successive generations of women like me had lived, the small circumference of self to be had in a hardly-on-the-map hometown. It had taken all of the alcohol in the world to bring that out of me, but as soon as I was sober, I wanted it back, my little circle of me.

"I don't know if *trapped* is the word," I said.

"Limited, then," he said.

"What could it matter now?" I asked. "We're a family."

And that was it. The end of the reckoning.

When my son was in the NICU there was a complicated sequence of events that had to take place every time I re-entered the hospital. I had to page the nurse's desk with a secret code, walk through an Escher-worthy sequence of stairways and hallways, submit identification and documentation, sign consent forms, douse myself to the elbows in antibacterial foam, scrub my nailbeds, don scrubs and a face mask, and then I could stand next to the oversized Tupperware container in which Will dozed, swaddled. I would be permitted to hold him on a limited basis. A thin white line delivered my breastmilk to his stomach via his nose. I slept in a pink vinyl chair that was designed to be easy to clean but hard to sleep in. And then I'd get so exhausted and depraved that I'd go home and fall into a black sleep and have to start the sequence of events again.

I thought about those days as I signed-in to see Noah. This was the second time in my life that my life was conducted in two wholly distinct fields: home and hospital. Only this time, I wouldn't be going home with a bouncing boy; instead, I'd be going home a widow. It was depressing, but only if I slowed down long enough to let it register anew. Mostly, I barged around avoiding this fact. When I got to the room, a giant was standing over him. My impossibly tall son, who had arrived unannounced.

"Why are you here?" I asked as I flung down my bags and hugged him.

He laughed, hugged. "Did I forget to get your permission?"

I smacked him lightly on the shoulder. "You know what I mean. I didn't expect you."

Noah was sleeping. It was usually this way. We had learned that he didn't give a shit if we woke him, so we didn't bother to keep the volume down. We talked about Will's travel here to Athens. He had to fly into a city a few hours away and rent a car and then drive and it was a whole pain in the ass to park in a college town, but he said he found a great spot and was going to camp there for a while, so we could use the rental if we needed to get back to the house quickly. And then I asked him, "So, why are you here? I thought we talked about the timing."

"Mom," he said. He glanced at Noah, who was still deep in sleep. "Now is the time."

It hit me hard, a car dropped on my head. Noah had called Will. That was the only way he would know

103

that now was *now*. And the reason he knew it was *now*
and I didn't know it was *now*—despite the fact that I was
the one manning the fort—was that I was afraid of now.

"You didn't think I could handle it," I said. "The
two of you decided for me that I couldn't do it."

"Mom," he said. He ushered me into a seat. I
looked up at him, this giant man who was somehow also
my tiny son, born too many weeks too early. "We both
knew you could handle it. We didn't want you to have
to handle it."

I still felt blindsided and estranged—on the outside
of this inside—so I asked him if I could be alone with
his father and he silently agreed and disappeared to the
cafeteria. When you meet the man you marry when
you're a teen and you never divorce and you live pretty
much happily ever after together it can seem as though
the line between your young self and your older woman
self is a straight and a clear one. Perhaps that's why the
middle can fall out of the thing in your thinking. The
impossible gap between the girl and the widow. Perhaps
dreaming was a way of negotiating the trauma of the
straight line that ends, but must go on. *How can this be?*
How can I go on without you?

I draped myself over Noah in the hospital bed and
talked to him in his ear. I knew he might not pass that
day. He might still be with me tomorrow. But the end
was very near now. *Now, now, now.*

"I talked to Kara today," I said. I talked to him like I would have talked to him if I'd just set a plate full of roast beef at his place at the table. We liked to chat about our days over meat. "She said she hoped you'd pull through and I called her a fucking flake."

If he heard me, he'd know I was embroidering the truth (I never dropped the F-bomb in public and I habitually defended Kara to the others even though I didn't particularly like her) and he'd play along a little in his mind. "Really?" he might ask if he were able. "And what did she say?"

"She didn't say anything, of course," I said. "She knew I was right."

Were he able, he might have laughed and we would have gone on and on like that. Forever. But he was not able. He was in the process of leaving me. He'd left me once before, but our time together was finally coming to an end.

"You know something, sweetness," I said. "You're a real pain in my ass, but I love you."

They were the precise words he'd once used on me to lift me over and beyond the crises of the past—the cheating and the miscarriages and the anxieties and the disappointments and the illness—and they were the last words he heard spoken on this earth, if he heard them at all. When Will returned to the room, Noah was gone. The nurses allowed us to cling to him until he was cold and then, with their kind and professional hands, we were shuttled into the next phase of our being. Still a family, but a family with a loss in its center. We sat weeping in Will's car together and then he drove me home. The house was the same old house, a big shambling bank of rickety boards. Heading up the steep drive could feel like launching into the sky. *Chauffeur*, I thought, *where do we go from here?*

It took me time to muster up the courage to speak with Trace again. Not because I feared we'd fall into each other's arms and then self-immolate in beery small-town fashion, but because the dreams had shown me deeper, uncontrolled aspects of myself that I wasn't entirely certain I could master and still didn't fully understand. Months and months passed and there was this strange energy sitting there, unresolved. Plus, Trace had been distinctly *un*invited to the funeral Noah had arranged. This was a sore spot for Will and probably, I reasoned, for his father. But we did it exactly the way Noah had wanted it done. I wasn't confident I could handle the complexities involved in apologizing for the awkwardness of my husband's dying wishes. Still, I didn't want Trace to feel scorned.

In the end, he was kind enough to make it easy for me by getting my birthday wrong and mailing me a card. "I thought it was in October," he said on the phone, and I assured him it was still in December. "Really?" he asked. "I had a distinct memory of eating cake in a big heat wave."

"Maybe we did eat cake when it was hot once, but it wasn't my birthday."

"Really?" he asked again. "I could have sworn."

He let a pause happen and I could hear him lighting a cigarette on the other end of the line. I thought about chiding him. Hadn't he seen what Noah had been through with his cancer? But then I realized he was only smoking because he was nervous. "Did you maybe send the card because you wanted to check up on me?"

"If I did, would that be so bad?"

"You don't need an excuse to talk to me. We're still family, you know."

He took some deep breaths and then laid it on me. "Sister, I don't know if you know this. Maybe you do and you wouldn't say. But Noah called me at the end. Right before he passed."

"Oh, God," I said. "Did he tell you he was going to haunt you?"

Trace didn't seem to know what to say to that. He stuttered a bit and then dismissed the idea as a dumb joke I was trying and failing to make. "He told me he forgave me. And I was angry at first, you know? I was like, *you* forgive *me*? You've poked at me for decades. But then I realized he needed to let it go and so I let him."

"Why are you telling me this?"

"I'm telling you this because I need to forgive you too. I need to let it go."

"Forgive me? For what?"

I ran through all of my sins in my head—original to last Saturday. All of the sordid fantasies I'd entertained. *Could he see the dreams somehow?* I thought, weirdly. *Did he know?*

"I'm not one for deep conversations. I'm putting it out there because it needs to be said. I forgive you. I forgive you for all of it."

I will admit I was angry. I hung up and threw the phone against the wall. Three days later, I had a new phone. I used it to text him. *Thank you for saying what you said. It means a lot.* At first I was only thanking him to avoid further awkwardness, to have it over and done with. And then I was out in the yard, watching one dog or another run the grass dead along the fenceline. There was a chill in the air and I knew the weather would turn fully soon. I'd need to drag the patio furniture into the garage, layer tarps over the more fragile plantings. There would be salt to buy for the drive. Maybe, while I was thinking about it and had the energy, I'd go ahead and roll up a garden hose or two. A few months earlier, I would have grieved over the aloneness of such tasks, tasks that would have been a cooperative effort in years past. Now, I knew how to process them without also courting a leveling surge of grief. What exactly that might have to do with Trace's decision to offer his forgiveness, I couldn't say, but I knew that I could live now on my own. And so that's what I did.

About the Author:

Sarah Anne Strickley is the author of *Fall Together* (Gold Wake Press, 2018). She's a recipient of a National Endowment for the Arts Creative Writing fellowship, the *Copper Nickel* Editors' Prize for Prose,  and other honors. Her stories and essays have appeared in *Oxford American*, *A Public Space*, *Witness*, *Harvard Review*, *Gulf Coast*, *The Southeast Review*, *The Normal School*, *Ninth Letter*, *Copper Nickel*, *storySouth* and elsewhere. She's a graduate of the Iowa Writers' Workshop and earned her PhD from the University of Cincinnati. She's an Assistant Professor of creative writing at the University of Louisville and serves as faculty editor of *Miracle Monocle*.

About the Publisher:

Summer Camp Publishing is an independent press specializing in brief works of large ambition. For author and press correspondence, classroom copies, speaking engagement inquires and information about existing and upcoming publications, please visit us online at http://www.summercamppublishing.com.